D0849519

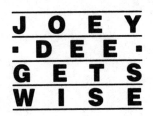

JOEY DEE GETS WISE

A novel of Little Italy

LOUISA ERMELINO

St. Martin's Press
NEW YORK

Portions of this work have previously appeared in *NYU Magazine* and *The Malahat Review*.

Design by Glen Edelstein

Library of Congress Cataloging-in-Publication Data

Ermelino, Louisa.
    Joey Dee gets wise / Louisa Ermelino.
        p.   cm.
    ISBN 0-312-05451-3
    PS3555.R55J6   1991
    813'.54—dc20   90-49191
                                                              CIP

First Edition: February 1991
10 9 8 7 6 5 4 3 2 1

FOR CARLO, AMO, AND BIG LOU

PROLOGUE

When the baby was born, the mother asked the midwife to take the afterbirth outside.

"I can't," Alfonsina whispered. "You got a girl. Don't you want her to stay home?"

The mother didn't. Armando was somewhere in the streets, already drunk, angry that he'd made a buttonhole.

"Take it outside," the mother said. "This is America."

"I can't," Alfonsina said. "Men go out of the house. No one wants a man who stays home, a *ricchione*, under his mother's skirts. But a woman . . . If the afterbirth stays in the house, the woman stays in the house. You know that. A woman belongs in the house," she told the mother. "Let me put it down the toilet."

"Take it," the mother said again, "and dig a hole."

Alfonsina looked out the window at the lines of laundry. "Don't ask me to do this," she said. "I'm too old now. I can't dig a hole so deep the dogs don't find it."

The mother leaned forward. "Take the money from the jar in the kitchen and get someone to help you. Pay them to dig a place and don't say nothing."

"But if someone sees?" Alfonsina said. "Everybody knows you got a girl. And Armando? What about Armando?"

Alfonsina pulled a handkerchief from under the sleeve of her dress and twisted it in her fist. The baby cried and the mother turned away.

"Take her," Alfonsina said. "Take your baby and forget this. You got a girl. Girls are always with you. You'll get more babies. You'll get sons."

The mother would not look. She would not take the baby. She would not be persuaded.

"Trouble," Alfonsina said. "You make trouble with this thing, I can tell you."

She went to the kitchen to find the jar. It was behind the tins of flour on the shelf covered in yellow oilcloth.

Alfonsina put the afterbirth in a rag and wrapped it in newspaper. She tied the package with a string. The things people want in America, she thought.

Downstairs in the yard, Alfonsina remembered the baby had no name, and she walked back up the stairs. The mother was sitting at the kitchen table. The sweater over her shoulders had no buttons. She was drinking wine.

"The baby has no name," Alfonsina said.

"Take some wine," the mother said, going to the shelf to get a glass.

"And the baby's name?" Alfonsina said.

"When I go to the priest . . ."

"No," said Alfonsina. "I need it for the legal paper. This is America."

The mother poured the wine. "I don't know."

Alfonsina shook her head. "I come another time, but you don't wait too long. I need it for the paper."

She finished the wine and got up to go. "Don't forget," she

said. "You tell Armando no if he tries to bother you. You just had a baby. You tell him Alfonsina says he can't bother you."

"He won't listen," the mother said.

"Ah," said Alfonsina. "If it was Donna Vecchio said it, he would listen. They all listen to Donna Vecchio. It falls off when they don't listen. You should have called Donna Vecchio for your baby."

Alfonsina opened the door. She was already in the hall when the mother touched her arm. The mother pointed to the package wrapped in newspaper.

"You swear to me, Alfonsina," she said.

"Yes, yes, I swear. Rest now or the milk won't come. And then where will you be? You and your mixed-up baby?"

When Alfonsina had gone, the mother picked up the baby. The baby was bound in strips of bed sheet, beginning under the arms and pulled tightly to the toes, where Alfonsina had tied a knot.

"You have to do this," she had told the mother, "to make the legs grow straight."

But now the mother unwrapped the baby and let the legs kick free. She sat in the chair by the window that looked out into the yard and the lines of laundry.

She undid her dress. She wasn't worried about the milk. With the other baby, the one that couldn't swallow, there had been so much milk that when the baby died, no one could make the milk go away . . . until Donna Vecchio had come with her powers of *afattura* and a paste of olive oil and parsley. Donna Vecchio would be angry that she wasn't called for this baby.

The mother tried not to be afraid. This was America. She tried not to be afraid of Donna Vecchio. She tried not to be afraid of Armando.

Armando, who had come to her brother's house in Brooklyn one day to ask for her.

"Yes," her brother's wife had said.

"Who is he?" her brother had asked his wife that night when she told him.

"He's Genovese," his wife had said.

"But what does he do?" her brother had asked.

"He's Genovese, I told you," the wife had said. "What are you worried about? The Genovese always make a dollar. The undertaker, the butcher, all Genovese."

"She's a child," her brother had said.

"She's old enough."

Armando, had come and taken her from her brother's house in Brooklyn with the front yard and brought her here to the building across from the horse stables. She had carried her own things.

Once she had gone to her brother, and her brother had said he would kill Armando with a knife.

But this was America.

Could she see her brother in jail because of Armando? She had come back alone to the building across from the horse stables.

The mother sat in the chair by the window with her baby. She heard the men coming home from work and the children called in from the street. She heard them on the stairs and smelled the cooking from their open doors.

Outside the window the laundry had disappeared. Empty clotheslines crisscrossed the yard. The mother looked out the window to where her girl would go, not to hang laundry, and she waited for Armando.

Armando, who would come home and shout that there was no fire, that there was no food. He would try to bother her or he would be too drunk. He would not remember about the baby. She would not tell him.

If the sounds got too loud and the women got frightened, they would call the police. The police would come to the building across from the horse stables. They had come before, because this was America.

The men would not interfere. Behind the door was Armando's house. It would be the women who would call the police, and the police would come and make her open the door. They would make her let Armando in his house.

The men would nod. It was Armando's house. The women would stand in the hall with their heads covered. Some things do not change.

In the morning the baby cried. The mother went into the yard for wood to make a fire. She ate bread and coffee and sat in the chair by the window with her baby.

A policeman came. He asked the mother to come with him. She wrapped the baby, covered her shoulders, and followed him to where they showed her Armando with no blood in his face.

"An accident," the policeman said, "a fight. We don't know. Do you know?" he asked.

"I don't know," she told him.

"We'll find out," he said.

She knew they wouldn't.

When she came home, the women were waiting for her. They were waiting on the stoops and they were waiting by their open doors.

"Armando is dead," she told them.

Alfonsina came. She called out to the Virgin and Santa Rosalina. "I heard," she said. "I just heard about Armando." She took a package wrapped in newspaper from under her skirts. "I brought it back," she said. "We can do it now. We can flush it down the toilet now. You don't need no more trouble."

"Give it to me," the mother said.

Alfonsina crossed herself. She swore she would say nothing, and she left the mother and the baby and the package wrapped in newspaper that she had carried under her skirts.

Armando came into the house that night in the undertaker's box. He lay on the white satin inside the box in the black suit he was married in. The people came and gave the mother money folded inside envelopes. The women whispered and shook their heads. She was young to have no husband. Why didn't she cry?

The men standing in the corners talked of other things. Some of them watched her too closely. She was young, they thought. She would get lonely. Maybe, when some time had passed . . .

The paid mourners in black shawls moaned over Armando's body. They moved back and forth over him, shaking water blessed by the priest from their fingers. The water made damp spots on Armando's black wedding suit.

Donna Vecchio came. When Donna Vecchio came, everything stopped. Her hair was done in marceled waves. Her hairdresser lived in her house. Donna Vecchio had large breasts and short, bent legs. The envelope she gave the mother smelled of lavender.

"I'm sorry for your trouble," Donna Vecchio said. "And how is the baby?"

"Do you want to see her?" the mother said.

"The baby isn't mine," Donna Vecchio said. "You didn't call me for this baby. She isn't one of mine."

"But she is," the mother said. "She will have your name, Carolina. You will baptize her, and you will be her *gummara*."

Donna Vecchio smiled and held out her hand for the mother to kiss.

The rows of borrowed chairs were empty. The mother sat alone. She would sit all night to watch for Armando's spirit. When the spirit of the dead leaves, it looks for a sleeping body to enter. It enters through the mouth.

The mother wouldn't sleep, but would sit all night with Armando, with the sound of the ice melting into the pan underneath his black box. She would not let the baby sleep.

Underneath Armando's body was a block of ice, and underneath Armando's head, underneath the white satin pillow, was the package wrapped in newspaper.

And tomorrow they would bury Armando. They would put him in the ground with the afterbirth of the baby, in a hole so deep the dogs don't find it.

ONE

Sonny Magro's body was in the street when the ladies went to church. The ladies had on big hats and wore them tilted to one side. Sonny Magro's blood made a pool in the gutter along the curb. It was August and hot.

Joey Dee, Mikey Bats and Carmine stood on the corner in their best clothes. They went into the church late, after the Mass had started, and they stood in the back.

In the church the ladies put their heads together behind their prayer books. They whispered to one another underneath the big hats.

It wasn't the blood in the street. It wasn't that Sonny Magro had been killed in a way they had never seen a man killed before, but that Sonny Magro was a working guy, a pants presser, Joey Dee would say, and today was Sunday.

When Father Giannini let out the Mass, everyone crowded onto the church steps, wanting to stay near the top, wanting to see better into the street where Sonny Magro's body had been.

Joey Dee stood off to the side, leaning against the railing that the ladies would hold on to when the church steps were wet. He was standing alone when Vito Santero came next to him and pulled on his arm.

Vito Santero was crying with his mouth wide open and no sound coming out. He wiped his nose with the sleeve of his coat, and when he looked at Joey Dee, his bad eye rolled in his head.

Vito Santero was slow. He was born that way, the ladies said, but Joey Dee knew the truth.

Standing on the church steps now with Vito Santero made Joey Dee think about Sister Agnes, but then he put an arm around Vito and thought about getting snot on his suit. Joey Dee hoped he wouldn't.

"C'mon, Vito," he said. "What's the matter with you? Why you crying?"

Vito Santero opened his eyes wide. "I seen," he said. "I seen what happened to Sonny Magro."

Joey Dee pushed him when he said this. Vito Santero slipped off the step onto the one below. "What are you talking about?" Joey Dee said. "What the hell are you saying? You didn't see nothing."

"I did. I seen what happened." Vito Santero grabbed Joey Dee's arm. He put his mouth up close to Joey Dee's ear. "They killed Sonny Magro last night. It was late. He gets home late. They threw him off the roof. They killed him and threw him off the roof." Vito Santero pointed across the street, at Sammy One-eye's building, the building Vito lived in, the building Sonny Magro lived in before he was killed. "I seen them," Vito said.

Joey Dee and Vito Santero were alone on the church steps. There were footprints down below on the sidewalk made in Sonny Magro's blood. The ladies had moved across the street into Canapa's to buy rolls and crumb cake cut into squares. Joey Dee didn't want to hear what Vito Santero was saying.

Joey Dee thought about being too grown a man to be in church anymore, even in the back. He made the others go, Mikey Bats and Carmine. They would be glad if he told them they could stop. He looked for them. They usually waited for him after church, but today they were gone.

Vito Santero pulled on Joey Dee's arm. "I was going to put out the ashcans," Vito was saying. "My mother got mad, me putting them out so late, having to go down so late. 'Shit him,' my mother said. 'Shit Sammy One-eye and his lousy couple of bucks. He stinks on ice,' my mother said. So I didn't. I didn't put them out."

"So how the hell did you end up on the roof?"

"I went to see the birds, to stay with the birds," Vito said.

"I told you to leave the birds alone at night. I told you, Vito, once they're inside you gotta leave them alone. You don't do like I tell you, I'm not gonna let you clean out the boxes no more. I'm not gonna let you take care of them."

"I love the birds, Joey. You know that. I don't do nothing to bother the birds. I like to go up there and see them. I like that sound they make. I like how warm it gets in there."

"Jesus, Vito, it's August. It's dying out and you gotta go sit in a pigeon coop to get warm?"

"I open the little windows like you showed me, so it stays nice in there. I take care of the birds, Joey. You got some nice birds."

Joe Funz had given Joey Dee the birds when his wife died and he went to Staten Island to live with his daughter. Joe Funz's daughter told him to leave his dirty habits in New York. She meant his birds, and Joe Funz knew this, so he gave everything to Joey Dee: the birds, the coops, the feed that was left. It was all up on Sammy One-eye's roof. Joe Funz had some of the best birds around. He had some that had carried messages in the war.

"You don't have to be up there at night," Joey Dee told Vito. "How many times do I have to say it?"

"But that's how come I seen what happened. They came up

the roof. Three of them, with Sonny Magro. Nicky Mole, he was there. I could see them good."

Joey Dee looked down at the tips of his Siegel Brothers shoes. Vito Santero stood in front of him on the step below, bobbing up and down, waving his hands.

"And you know what they did?" Vito said.

"Listen, Vito. I don't want to hear it. . . . I gotta go."

Vito Santero held on to Joey Dee's arm. "They killed him," Vito said. He twisted up his face and shook his hands in front of him. He put one hand around his neck and choked himself. He opened his eyes wide. The bad eye, the left one, rolled in his head. "They put the rope around his neck, Joey. His tongue was hanging out. Then they took off his pants and they cut him, they cut off his . . ." Vito Santero lowered his voice. "You know what I mean," he said, moving closer to Joey Dee, stretching up, his mouth at Joey Dee's ear. "They cut it off and they put it . . ." Vito squeezed his eyes shut. "They put it in his mouth."

Joey Dee thought that he would throw up on the church steps and that the ladies would step in it and make footprints on the sidewalk down below. Joey Dee thought about Vegas, in the desert. It was a place he wanted to go.

"You should see the blood, Joey. The street's nothing. It's all up the roof. You wanna go see?" Vito Santero was excited telling this to Joey Dee, Joey Dee listening. "All that blood," Vito was saying, "because they cut it off. The rope don't make you bleed. I know that." What he was saying didn't mean anything to Vito Santero. It was that he was saying it, all of it, to Joey Dee, telling his secret to Joey Dee, standing with him alone on the church steps, just him and Joey Dee.

It was hot standing on the church steps. The sun was on the side of the street where the church was and Joey Dee took off his tie and folded it twice so it wouldn't wrinkle when he put it in his pocket.

"Why don't you shut up, Vito?" Joey Dee said. "You're supposed to be stupid, remember? How come you know so much?"

"I'm not stupid, Joey," Vito said. "They didn't see me, did they? Everybody thinks those guys know everything, but they ain't so smart. Nicky Mole ain't so smart." Vito Santero twisted up his face. He could do that, twist up his face so that his mouth and nose and one eye, the bad one, came together. "Sister Agnes used to call me stupid. You remember Sister Agnes, Joey? You remember her?"

When Vito said this, he opened his mouth wide and cried with no sound coming out. Vito always cried with no sound. His mother said it was enough to drive her crazy, that and the bad eye that rolled in his head.

Joey Dee took Vito Santero's arm and squeezed it hard. "Listen," he said. "How do you know they didn't see you?"

"I was with the birds, Joey. I told you. You don't listen. I heard somebody coming and I got inside. I closed the door and stayed inside with the birds. I stayed still. I didn't come down for a long time. My mother, she didn't know where to look."

Joey Dee let go of Vito Santero's arm. "You listen to me," he said. "You go home and you forget what you saw and you forget you told me anything. Sonny Magro's dead. It don't matter what you saw unless you want to be next."

Joey Dee went down the church steps two at a time. He didn't hold on to the railing.

Vito started after him. "Where you going, Joey? Where you going?"

Joey Dee stopped. "I'm going home," he said, "and lie to my mother. I'm gonna tell her I took communion and sat in the front of the church. She's gonna be so happy she's gonna kiss me on the mouth and feed me crumb cake from her fingers."

"Yeah, Joey, yeah?" Vito said. He followed Joey Dee down the street and Joey Dee let him, but when they passed the cafe where Nicky Mole stood outside and Vito Santero started pulling on Joey Dee's arm and whispering in his ear, Joey Dee pushed him into the next doorway and held him against the wall.

"This time I mean it, Vito," Joey Dee said. "Go home and keep your mouth shut like I told you."

Joey Dee didn't go down that Sunday afternoon to look for Mikey Bats and Carmine, and he didn't go up the roof to fly the pigeons. He believed Vito Santero. He believed what Vito had told him about the blood up the roof.

It rained that night and for days afterward. It rained as though it were part of a plan to wash the blood from the roof. It rained for all the days of Sonny Magro's wake.

Everyone came to Sonny Magro's wake. Angelina Lombardi, so fat she hadn't left the house in fifteen years, came to Sonny Magro's wake. It took four of her sons-in-law to get her down the stairs. The fifth had a bad back, and besides, he reminded her, he was waiting on a compensation case.

The four sons-in-law carried Angelina Lombardi down the stairs in a kitchen chair and over to Gambino's Funeral Parlor. Everyone was there for Sonny Magro's wake. Only Donna Vecchio the midwife had had more people at her wake, and she had thrown a curse from her deathbed onto anyone who didn't come.

Everyone came to wakes to see the flowers and to see the people. The women sat on folding chairs facing the coffin. The men stood lined up against the wall, or crowded near the coatracks, blocking the entrance.

Everyone came to see what the dead was wearing and what the box was like. They counted the roses in December. They pressed the hands and kissed the faces of the living and measured their grief. They watched for feuds and alliances.

Coming to wakes guaranteed the turnout at your own. The thought of Gambino's Funeral Parlor filled with people and flowers made death seem worth it. To be laid out in a room with empty chairs was the nightmare.

But there were wakes and there were wakes.

Sonny Magro was having a wake.

*   *   *

Joey Dee hated wakes, but he went to Sonny Magro's wake the way he went to all the others. Mikey Bats and Carmine were standing against the wall when he got there. There wasn't an empty chair. Joey Dee put his hand in his pants pocket.

"Save it," Carmine said. "The widow's not taking places. Something, huh? When was the last time you went to a wake that it didn't cost you a sawbuck?"

Joey Dee took his hand out of his pocket and shrugged his shoulders to straighten his suit jacket. "You got no respect, Carmine," he said. He would have smiled but he was too nervous. Wakes made him nervous.

Joey Dee walked up the side aisle to the coffin. He had to wait his turn. Someone handed him a holy card with the Madonna's picture on one side, Sonny Magro's on the other. Sonny Magro's first name was Salvatore. Joey Dee hadn't known that. The card was edged in gold and sealed in plastic, the best Gambino's had to offer.

When Joey Dee knelt in front of Sonny Magro's coffin, he didn't look in. He never did. He looked down at his hands folded on the velvet kneeler. The sweat started inside his collar.

Poor bastard, he thought, all dressed up and no place to go.

The widow sat in the first chair. Joey Dee waited his turn again. She watched as he came over to her.

"I'm sorry for your trouble, Carolina," Joey Dee said. It was what he always said at wakes. His mother had taught him.

When he bent down to say this, Carolina Magro took his face in her hands and kissed him, once on each cheek. She smiled then, and with her thumb wiped away the stain of lipstick she had left too near his mouth.

"Lipstick," the ladies said. "Him not cold and her mouth painted. Back when," the ladies said, "a widow didn't wash, she didn't change her sheets." The ladies shook their heads. They arranged the veils on their black hats.

"She's young," Angelina Lombardi said. "These are different times."

"What do you know?" the ladies said to her. "You sitting in your house for fifteen years."

"I sit by the window," Angelina Lombardi said. "I know."

When Father Giannini came to say the rosary, the men left. They stood outside in groups on the sidewalk. They loosened their collars and smoked cigarettes. Bits of tobacco stuck to their bottom lips.

"What do you think?" Carmine said. He stood with Mikey Bats and Joey Dee, one foot on the stone urn where Gambino sometimes planted geraniums. "Looks pretty good for a stiff, no?"

"Jesus, Carmine," Mikey Bats said. "You sound like my mother. She's always coming home from some dead saying how good he looks. How the hell do you look good when you're dead?"

Carmine lit a cigarette. He put his face down close to the match. "C'mon, you know what I mean. The way they found Sonny Magro and all. It ain't right he looks so good. Old Man Gambino ain't such a talent he makes deads look so good. Tell me, Joey, am I right?"

Joey Dee shrugged. He was thinking how much he hated wakes. He was thinking about Sonny Magro's blood in the street and about Carolina Magro's mouth.

Mikey Bats shifted from one foot to the other. "For Chrissakes, Carmine," he said. "Why you always going in circles? Why don't you say what you mean? You're gonna be sitting on a park bench with the neighborhood ladies pretty soon, you don't watch out."

Carmine ignored Mikey Bats and faced Joey Dee. "What I'm telling you is that Sonny Magro looks so good because Old Man Gambino didn't do the job. Some guy came in from Detroit. Some hotshot who fixes up stiffs who didn't die so nice. And did you see the suit? Sonny Magro alive never had a suit half that good. He's wearing a Sulka tie, for Chrissakes. I bet Gambino takes it off before he closes the box."

Mikey Bats hit Carmine's arm. "And who?" he said. "Who got this guy to come from Detroit?"

Carmine turned and looked at Mikey Bats. "Who do you think, Mikey? The same guy who's paying for the funeral. Who else could get a guy to come from Detroit?"

"You're crazy," Mikey Bats said. "Crazy Carmine. You know they call you that?"

Joey Dee got between them. He tried to look bored. Mikey Bats stepped back. "You're always looking for an angle, Carmine," Mikey Bats said over Joey Dee's shoulder. "Maybe Nicky Mole did go for the funeral like they're saying, but so what? The wise guys are good that way, and Nicky Mole's the best. Remember Gracie Paretti's kid that got burned? Remember he paid all the bills to fix the kid's face?"

"That was different," Carmine said. "That was a kid. Why should he make such a big deal for a pants presser like Sonny Magro?"

"The guy's dead," Joey Dee said. "Don't you have no respect?"

"You're the one always calling guys that," Carmine said.

"What's being a pants presser got to do with it?"

"Don't you see? Pants pressers don't get themselves killed like that, and they don't wear no Sulka ties in their coffins. There's something else going on."

"What about Josie?" Mikey Bats said. "She's gotta remember her father messed up like that in the street? It was a hell of a way to go, and nobody knows why. Maybe Nicky Mole did it for Josie, so she could remember him nice, all dressed up, like he's sleeping."

Carmine rolled his eyes. "Give me a break, Mikey, please."

"Where was Josie? I didn't see her," Joey Dee said.

"Up the house," Mikey Bats told him. "She's been up there since Sunday. The doctor gave her pills. She pulled out her hair when she saw her father in the street. Big fistfuls of hair, the ladies said."

"Josie was always a weirdo," Carmine said. He was surprised when Joey Dee caught his jacket collar in his hands.

"What do you mean, weirdo?" Joey Dee said. "Why you calling her that?"

Carmine put up his hands, palms open. "I'm sorry, Joey," he said. "You hot for Josie Magro or something? I'm sorry, OK? I didn't mean nothing."

Joey Dee let go. He put his hands in his pockets. "Forget it," he said.

Carmine and Mikey Bats didn't know about him and Josie. Nobody did, because Joey Dee wasn't a guy who talked.

Mikey Bats put an arm around Joey Dee's shoulder. "So what do you think about Sonny Magro?" he asked him. "You ain't said a word."

"What's to say? He looks pretty good for a guy who was choked to death."

Carmine looked at Joey Dee. "Choked? There was all that blood. What makes you say Sonny Magro was choked?"

Joey Dee backed off the curb, one foot in the street. "I don't know," he said. "I thought he was choked."

"Where'd you get that, Joey?"

"Why you getting all hot and bothered?" Joey Dee said. "Choked, not choked, who cares? Sonny Magro's dead and he looks good laid out. So what? This place stinks no matter what you look like."

Mikey Bats shook his head. He looked confused. "What place stinks, Joey? Gambino's? What's wrong with Gambino's?"

"Gambino carries you up them stairs in a basket," Joey Dee said, "like a pile of dirty laundry."

"You got someplace better you want to go? With the Irish, maybe?" Carmine shuffled his feet. He danced a jig. "Who's gonna come? Your mother?"

"No, your mother," Joey Dee said.

"Leave my mother out of it," Carmine said. "She wouldn't be caught dead in no donkey funeral parlor."

Joey Dee thought Carmine would take a stance, mothers

being sacred, but instead he waved to one of Angelina Lombardi's sons-in-law standing nearby and walked over to talk to him.

Joey Dee didn't tell Mikey Bats and Carmine that he didn't want anybody coming to his wake, standing around like this, talking about how good he looked dead. He didn't want anybody to see him like Sonny Magro, all dressed up and no place to go. He didn't tell them, his friends, because he wasn't a guy who talked.

The rosary was over. The ladies came out of the funeral parlor, down the stairs to the sidewalk where the men waited. Inside, Carolina Magro would be saying good night to her husband. She would be bending over the coffin to kiss his mouth. If the ladies could see, she would do this.

But Carolina would wait until the ladies couldn't see, Joey Dee thought, until they had all followed Father Giannini outside. She would wait and stand a certain way, and then to be sure, just in case, she would bend over the coffin and pretend to kiss her husband's mouth.

Sonny Magro was buried on a Friday. At his funeral Mass the altar boys had brilliant black shoes that showed under the white skirts of their cassocks. Fernando ("Nicky Mole") Malevento had sent Fat Frankie to ask Father Giannini which boys were serving Sonny Magro's Mass. To buy them shoes, Fat Frankie told Father Giannini, so they wouldn't stand on the altar in the dirty sneakers they wore to play stickball in the street. And, Fat Frankie added, the donor wished to remain anonymous.

Father Giannini said it was too generous of Don Malevento, as was the gold chalice donated in Sonny Magro's name. Father Giannini accepted these gifts with great thanks on behalf of the widow. There are many ways into heaven, he would remind anyone who asked.

No one was supposed to know about the shoes but Joey Dee knew. One of the altar boys was Carmine's kid brother, and Carmine told Joey Dee and Mikey Bats that when the kid came home with the shoes, his mother got crazy.

"She thought the kid was buying swag," Carmine said. "She knocked him all over the place trying to find out how he got them shoes, but he wouldn't talk. She finally got it out of him about going to Siegel Brothers with Fat Frankie and that the shoes were for Sonny Magro's funeral Mass. Then she tells him to take the shoes back and get the money. 'What's a kid like you doing with shoes like that?' she says. She tells him she'll polish his school shoes black so no one will know the difference. She says she'll get him a nice new pair on Orchard Street if he wants. She's feeding him all this and the kid's listening and then he just starts yelling. He says he don't want no cheap East Side pushcart shoes and if she makes him take the shoes back he'll rat. He'll tell Fat Frankie. He might even go inside the cafe and tell Nicky Mole."

Joey Dee had laughed, but Carmine just thought it was another strange thing connected to Sonny Magro's ending up dead on Sullivan Street on a Sunday morning. "You guys don't want to listen," he said, "but you'll see."

"See what?" Mikey Bats wanted to know. "It don't have nothing to do with none of us."

Joey Dee thought about Vegas. He wished he were there, in the desert, alone.

Sonny Magro's Mass was long and the schoolchildren sang it. The ladies, their hats black, veils down, kneeled when the altar boy rang the small gold bell. Carolina Magro stood. The ladies lined the pews behind her.

Sonny Magro's coffin was in the aisle outside the altar railing, covered with a white cloth. The ladies had sewn the cloth. They had embroidered HE IS THE RESURRECTION AND THE LIFE across it in scarlet thread.

Carolina Magro wore a black veil that covered her face and hung in folds past her throat. The veil was silk, and through its blackness the red of her mouth was startling.

The talk was of who had killed Sonny Magro and why. The ladies narrowed their eyes. Someone had killed Sonny

Magro and had left his body mutilated in the street, but the ladies would have said, if only someone had asked, that Carolina Magro had started to kill Sonny Magro from the day she married him in this church.

Carolina was alone in the first pew. Josie Magro was still up the house on pills. The ladies did not approve. Don't we all suffer? they said. Mrs. Pieri lost her only son under the bus. The Carluccis, all of them dead from the Spanish influenza, except the mother, who put her head in the oven and gassed the cat. Josie Magro should be here at her father's funeral, the ladies said. She should be here if only to make up for the red of her mother's mouth.

A row of black Cadillacs was waiting outside when the Mass ended. Mikey Bats said that when they buried his uncle in Florida the coffin and the Cadillacs were blue like the sky. Joey Dee told him to shut up.

They were going to the cemetery in Carmine's brother's car. They were supposed to give Carmine's mother a ride, but they left the church without looking for her.

Carmine moved the car into the line of cars that started at the church and went down and around the block. "Jesus," he said. "There's enough limousines for the whole neighborhood."

"I hope your mother gets to go in one," Joey Dee said.

"C'mon, Joey, do you really want to ride all the way to Calvary with my old lady in the car?"

"I don't even want to go," Mikey Bats said. "What do we have to go for?"

Joey Dee told him to shut up. Joey Dee wanted to go. The funeral was the end, he hoped. The ladies would talk and Carmine would go on for a while, but Sonny Magro's murder would pass into neighborhood mythology like everything else.

Then he saw Vito Santero on the corner of Sullivan Street watching the procession of cars with their headlights on. Vito was scratching his balls, which is what to do when a funeral procession passes.

"Look at Vito," Carmine said. "He's got a tie on for Sonny Magro. Let's pick him up and take him with us."

Joey Dee grabbed the wheel. "No," he said, "leave him alone."

"What's with you?" Carmine said. "We'll have some fun."

When Vito Santero saw Joey Dee was in the car, he started into the street. He twisted up his face, screwed up his mouth till it met his bad eye. He put his hand on the car door. "Joey," he said. "Hey, Joey. Joey!" Vito Santero pulled at the handle of the car door. The line of cars started to move.

Joey Dee looked straight ahead and told Carmine to keep going. Joey Dee said he didn't want to ride to the cemetery with some retard.

TWO

Joey Dee thought that after the funeral was maybe the time to get rid of Josie Magro. He liked her, but there were plenty of girls around not half bad-looking who would go his way. No one knew he was seeing her. Joey Dee had a reputation for being closemouthed. "Stone face," they called him behind his back. "Smiling Jack," they said.

Josie Magro would call for him in the hallway. She would stand in the hallway at the bottom of the stairs and yell up his name. Joey Dee's mother would stand by the sink in the kitchen and make faces when Josie Magro did this, when she heard Josie's voice in the hall, but she didn't ask him about her. She didn't want to know.

Josie Magro was complicated, Joey Dee told himself, what with a dead father and Carolina Magro for a mother.

When he thought of Carolina Magro, he remembered the line of gold at her ankle.

He had seen it when she followed Sonny Magro's coffin into church at the funeral Mass. It had been on her left ankle, he remembered, a gold bracelet under the black silk stocking.

Joey Dee had not stopped thinking about it through the whole Mass. He had looked at that gold bracelet on Carolina Magro's ankle the whole time she stood by the dug-out grave in Calvary where they had put Sonny Magro's coffin. It was all he saw when she stepped up to throw her flower on the coffin where Sonny Magro was, unless you believed Father Giannini, who said Sonny Magro was with God in heaven.

Father Giannini never talked about hell at funerals. He sent you up to God in heaven. He sent everyone up there, even Tommy California, who had put six bullets in the back of MoMo Birdy's head in the social club on Crosby Street. Father Giannini had sent Tommy California up to God in heaven at the biggest funeral the neighborhood had seen in thirty years.

Joey Dee thought it was really time for him to stop standing in the back of the church and maybe it was time for him to stop banging Josie Magro.

There were stories about Josie Magro, but they were really Carolina's stories. Carolina had always kept the ladies busy. For Josie, they had some sympathy. She was the manifestation of the sins of . . . an innocent. Not that it gave the ladies less to say.

"*Pazza*," they whispered. "Josie Magro? A little crazy in the head. Not that she can help it, born like that, a mother like that. Nervous," they said, "high-strung . . . no meat on her bones."

Joey Dee's mother listened to the stories and passed them on. She was a woman who saw ghosts under the stairs and kept a plaster Madonna in a goldfish bowl filled with water long after the goldfish had died. She said she had her reasons.

Joey Dee didn't want to listen to the stories. There were

things Joey Dee never wanted. He never wanted to be a pants presser like Sonny Magro or a horse like his father.

Josie, the ladies said, was what Carolina Magro didn't want. Carolina married Sonny Magro and some people said she had to, but it wasn't true. She had married Sonny Magro to make her mother happy and to get out of the factory where she packed figs and couldn't take a pee until lunchtime. She sat with sweaty little girls who wore printed aprons over their cheap dresses and talked about boyfriends and how they wouldn't.

Carolina would. She did. When she was seventeen she went with Tommy California, who was married, and old even then, and on his way down.

She was beautiful. In the neighborhood, beauty was a gift to the poor from God. What else could they get for nothing? It was given out sparingly, and it arrived unexpectedly, without reason, like the winning number passed along on street corners and in candy stores after the last horse race.

Carolina was the only child of Armando from Genova, who had appeared from nowhere and died drunk in the street not much later. Her mother always owed money to the Jew who sold door-to-door on Wednesdays.

What the mother had done for Carolina was to make Donna Vecchio, the midwife, her godmother and namesake. Because of this honor, Donna Vecchio put gold rings in Carolina's ears when she was baptized and promised that when Carolina married she would buy white satin for the dress.

Sometimes, Joey Dee had heard, for the festival of Saint Anthony, when the procession would stop in front of Donna Vecchio's door and wait there, the band playing, the saint high on the shoulders of six men, it would be Carolina who would climb the ladder to pin Donna Vecchio's gift onto the saint—a stiff, new one-hundred-dollar bill.

When Carolina married Sonny Magro, she wore a dress with seed pearls down the front. The dress had a long train and the veil was French lace. She was not excited, but her mother was.

Sonny Magro was tall and strong-looking and not too dark. He had a job with the post office. A pension, the mother said with pride. Carolina had no father and the beginnings of a reputation. She had been seen in back rooms sitting on Tommy California's lap. She wore dresses she couldn't afford.

Carolina and Sonny Magro were married in August. Tommy California made the connection for an apartment on Sullivan Street in Sammy One-eye's building. Tommy California was married and old and on his way down, but he was not a bad guy.

Some people said it was Tommy California's baby, but it wasn't. None of this mattered to Carolina. She didn't want anyone's baby.

Sonny Magro put linoleum on the kitchen floor of the apartment and washable paper on the walls.

Donna Vecchio put parsley in Carolina's womb and rubbed her belly with herbs she kept under oil. There were other ways, Donna Vecchio told Carolina, but not for the first. She wouldn't, not even for Carolina, who was her favorite goddaughter. Even this that she was doing was a great sin.

Sometimes, Donna Vecchio said, there were too many children, and a woman didn't care, but never for the first. Donna Vecchio shook her head of marceled waves. She pressed hard on Carolina's belly. Her gold bracelets were cold on Carolina's skin.

Josie Magro was born nine months to the day of Carolina's marriage to Sonny Magro. This was an omen for an easy birth, but Donna Vecchio, who had seen hundreds born, said she had never seen a baby so reluctant. She said there was something inside Carolina pulling the baby back into her.

Donna Vecchio, who could bring lovers back and turn

females to males in the womb, was helpless. Sonny Magro brought Carolina to the hospital at the end.

"Not now," they said. "It's too late."

Sonny Magro brought her home. Donna Vecchio threw up her hands. The baby's head appeared and disappeared. A foot came down, an arm, a hand, all of them pulled back up and into Carolina.

Josie Magro had spun in her mother's womb, Donna Vecchio said. She swore to it. She told the story only once but it was remembered and repeated where she couldn't hear.

Josie Magro was born after days and days. Donna Vecchio knit a hat to cover the baby's head and no one saw her without it.

The ladies argued among themselves.

"It's open at the top," some said.

"It comes to a point," said others.

Josie Magro was a skinny baby who wouldn't nurse. Josie Magro, the ladies decided, would be a little *pazza*.

These things they knew.

Joey Dee lay low for a while. There was nobody he wanted to see. He imagined Vito Santero waiting for him on Sullivan Street, outside Sammy One-eye's building, waiting to pull on his arm and whisper his story. He had decided to drop Josie Magro but he didn't want to see her. He didn't want to actually tell her what he had decided.

Joey Dee told his mother he was sick. His mother told this to Mikey Bats and Carmine when they came around. She told this to Joey Dee's father, too, but she warned Joey Dee that the old man wouldn't buy it for long.

When Joey Dee quit school, his father kept sending him back, until he said he was tired of wasting his time with a bum. He told Joey Dee if he quit school, he had to go to work. Joey Dee had made it until now without a steady job.

His father kept finding them and he kept losing them, but it was getting harder. The jobs were getting harder too.

His father had sent him out on every piece-of-shit job in New York City. Joey Dee carried hands of bananas off the boats from South America. He picked up garbage for the Mazzoni Brothers, who called it private carting. He waited tables in the strip joints on Third Street, serving champagne he made in the basement a few hours before.

For none of these jobs could he wear his Siegel Brothers shoes and his sharkskin suits. They were all sweaty jobs, and Joey Dee hated to sweat. He couldn't see what was so wrong about that. His mother agreed, but she couldn't convince the old man.

"Dress up on Sunday," his father said, "like everybody else."

"Shit you," Joey Dee didn't say.

Joey Dee stayed in bed for three days. His mother brought his food to him and tied a handkerchief soaked in alcohol around his head. His father said if Joey Dee's mother wasn't there, he would kill him with one hand.

Josie Magro came looking for Joey Dee. She stood in the hallway of the building where the stairs started and called up his name. Joey Dee didn't answer and his mother made like she didn't hear.

When the bed, the alcohol rag, and his mother got worse than the thought of the street, Joey Dee got out. His mother waited in the hallway while he took his bath in the kitchen tub and got his clean clothes out of the locked cedar closet. He had bought the closet the first time his number hit. He still played that number. It was Josie's birthday, 615, and it never hit again. He could stop playing it now that he was through with Josie Magro. It would be bad luck if he didn't.

Joey Dee said later he should have stayed in bed. He should have shaped up with Petey Black at Roger's Trucking. He should have left town. He should have let his old man kill him.

*   *   *

Fat Frankie was afraid.

When he had to tell Nicky Mole what he didn't want to hear, his stomach would rumble. So he would eat cream puffs in the shape of swans. He had just had two. He had put them whole into his mouth, one at a time. The powdered sugar was on his tie.

"You're sure?" Nicky Mole said.

Fat Frankie nodded. Benny Scar backed him up.

"The kid?" Nicky Mole said. "And the *stunade*?"

Fat Frankie nodded. There was custard on his cheek.

Nicky Mole tapped his coffee cup with his spoon. He didn't like to talk. He preferred to bang things. If Fat Frankie had been sitting close to him, instead of standing up, Nicky Mole would have hit him. He would have smacked him on the side of the head where the custard was stuck to his cheek.

"You tell the kid I want to see him," he said to Benny Scar. Fat Frankie had brought the bad news. Nicky Mole didn't want to talk to him anymore. He wanted to hit him, but Fat Frankie was standing up, too far away.

"Yeah, tell the kid to come by," Nicky Mole said to Benny Scar, "and keep an eye on the *stunade*."

Joey Dee was standing on the corner with the sun on his face when he got the word that Nicky Mole wanted to see him. Benny Scar brought it, and it had the power of the word from above, the word written in the sky in smoke from the back of an airplane, Joey Dee would say later.

Benny Scar came up to Joey Dee. He asked how he was doing and put his hands on Joey Dee like they were good friends.

"Nicky wants you to stop by the cafe," Benny Scar said. "A little talk, a cup of coffee . . ."

Joey Dee felt the sweat start inside his collar like it had when he knelt at Sonny Magro's coffin. "Sure," he said to Benny

Scar. Joey Dee tapped out a cigarette from his pack. Benny Scar lit a match. "Tell Nicky I'll come by," Joey Dee said.

Benny Scar smiled. It was hard to look at him, even when he smiled. His scar was a knotted line that went from his eyebrow to the corner of his mouth. It had not been a clean cut.

When he was sure Benny Scar was gone, when he had looked both ways up and down the street, Joey Dee went to find Vito Santero. He found him moving the ashcans in front of Sammy One-eye's building and came up behind him.

"Vito," he said.

Vito turned. He wiped the snot that was always hanging from the end of his nose across his coat sleeve and the back of his hand. Vito Santero wore his coat winter and summer. There were holes where the buttons used to be. Vito held out his hand to Joey Dee.

"For Chrissakes, Vito, don't you have a handkerchief? Can't your mother give you a handkerchief?"

"I didn't tell nobody, Joey. I didn't." Vito put his head down. He rolled an ashcan toward the alley between the buildings.

"You swear, Vito? Swear your mother gets cancer."

"I swear. I swear. Nobody knows about Sonny Magro on the roof," Vito shouted. His bad eye rolled in his head. He moved the ashcan back and forth like a giant toy.

"Shut up, Vito, and tell me," Joey Dee said. "Nobody? Nothing? It's important, Vito. This ain't kid stuff."

"Remember Sister Agnes, Joey?" Vito got quiet. He stood the ashcan up in front of him. His bad eye stopped moving. "Sister Agnes liked you," he said. "I wish she liked me the way she liked you."

Sammy One-eye's building was two doors up from the nun's house. Inside, Joey Dee remembered, was an underground tunnel that led to the school. Sister Agnes would meet Joey Dee in that tunnel, in one of its turns, and she would put her hands under his clothes.

That was how Sister Agnes liked Joey Dee.

She had not liked Vito Santero.

She had knocked him hard on the side of his head with the

piece of wood she kept by her desk. She had done this when he missed the word in the spelling bee.

Joey Dee remembered that blood had come out of Vito Santero's ear. He remembered that at three o'clock, when the mothers came, Sister Agnes had hid Vito in the coat closet. She had sent Joey Dee down to say Vito was staying after school.

Sister Agnes had hid Vito Santero in the coat closet until the blood stopped. Then she had washed his face and led him through the tunnel that ran under the street to the nuns' house. She had opened the door and sent him home.

That same year Father Giannini found Sister Agnes touching Joey Dee in the sacristy before Mass. Joey Dee was the altar boy. Sister Agnes had her hands under his cassock when Father Giannini came in.

Sister Agnes was sent to the motherhouse upstate and Father Giannini took Joey Dee into the confessional.

"Never," he told Joey Dee. "Never tell anyone."

"Never," Joey Dee told Vito Santero. "Never tell anyone."

Vito started crying and talking, but the words got mixed in his mouth and he wasn't saying anything Joey Dee could understand. Joey Dee gave him one of his handkerchiefs.

He always carried two, just in case, he said, but when Joey Dee put the extra white linen handkerchief in his pocket that morning, he wasn't thinking of Vito Santero but of Carolina Magro, of his white linen handkerchief pressed against her red mouth.

Vito took the handkerchief and put it carefully into his coat pocket. He ran his coat sleeve under his nose and over his face. He put his hands around his neck and wrestled himself to the ground. "I saw them, Joey. You know I saw them."

"OK, Vito, OK," Joey Dee said, pulling him up. "Forget it. Take it easy." Joey Dee was nervous. "Just don't say nothing, Vito. The same like I told you before."

Joey Dee patted Vito Santero on the side of the head, the side where Sister Agnes had hit him with the piece of wood and knocked his eye loose. He handed him his other white linen handkerchief. "Here, take it," he said. "It's OK."

Joey Dee went to church on Sunday and stood in the back. He lit a candle for Sonny Magro. They say the dead have power on earth. The souls in purgatory help the living because they need to be prayed up from the fire into heaven. It's just a matter of time. Joey Dee figured Sonny Magro must be in purgatory and not in heaven like Father Giannini said at the funeral. And if Sonny Magro was, then he'd be a good one to help out. He had started the whole mess, getting himself killed, only God knew why, on the roof of Sammy One-eye's building. If any soul in purgatory could help Joey Dee, it should be Sonny Magro.

Joey Dee lit two more candles, one for Vito Santero and one for Sister Agnes. Joey Dee did things a certain way. He knew bad things came in threes, so he always lit three candles at a time, hoping the good would balance the bad.

Sometimes, standing in the back of the church with the bells ringing and the dollar candles going, Joey Dee believed.

Standing on the corner after Mass, he told Mikey Bats and Carmine about Nicky Mole and Benny Scar.

"A sit-down," Carmine said. "I'm impressed. You and Nicky Mole, a sit-down."

"I didn't say a sit-down," Joey Dee said. "He wants to talk to me, that's all." Sit-down meant important. Joey Dee wanted to believe it was about nothing important.

"So what's a sit-down anyway?" Carmine said. "It's when you sit down and talk. Unless Nicky Mole is gonna make you stand up."

"Nah," Mikey Bats said, "Nicky's a gentleman."

Carmine looked at him. "You're serious, Mikey. You're really serious. Jesus."

Mikey Bats wanted to know exactly what Benny Scar had said.

"Yeah," Carmine said, "tell us, Joey. Did he say, 'Nicky wants the pleasure of your company'? Or, 'Nicky thinks you're a great guy'? Or . . ."

"Shut up," Joey Dee told him. "You think it's funny? You want to go for me?"

"Shit, Joey, I'm not saying it's funny, but what does Nicky Mole want with you? What's the big deal with you? Something going on we should know about?"

Joey Dee didn't answer. He didn't know himself. Joey Dee didn't want to think it had anything to do with Sonny Magro up the roof, but Carmine was right. What would Nicky Mole want with him?

The sweat started under Joey Dee's collar and he couldn't swallow. He would not have told Mikey Bats and Carmine about Benny Scar and Nicky Mole but they would have heard. He would have to go and see Nicky Mole, and when they found out they would ask him why he had gone and why he hadn't told.

Carmine, Joey Dee could see, was almost jealous. Carmine saw himself with Nicky Mole. He saw himself with his hat pulled low to one side. "Did the scar on Benny's face get red when he told you about the sit-down?" he asked Joey Dee. "I heard that's a dead giveaway. When Benny's out for blood, the scar turns red."

Joey Dee flicked his cigarette butt in the street. "I didn't notice," he said. "I'll check it out for you next time if I get the chance."

"You will," Carmine said. "Benny'll be around again."

"Shut the fuck up," Joey Dee said.

They hung out for a while but there was nothing to say. The street was empty. Canapa was taking the trays of crumb cake out of the window. He would sell it stale the next day for half price.

Joey Dee left first, and when he passed the church he thought he saw the stain of Sonny Magro's blood in the street.

THREE

Fernando ("Nicky Mole") Malevento was from the old country. This made him smart in ways and some said cruel. His reputation soared when he bit off the ear of a New York City police lieutenant who had spoken to him without respect.

He had come to New York with the clothes on his back and a white silk handkerchief tight in his hand. The trip and the handkerchief were his rewards for a service performed, a job well done.

Fernando Malevento murdered a man in the old country. He had murdered many men, but this time Fernando Malevento was arrested. He was told not to worry and he didn't. He knew he would be protected. He was dealing with honorable men.

Fernando Malevento was officially dead the day he should have arrived at the jail to begin his sentence. He was buried in a coffin with holes cut along its seams, and the local priest sent his soul to heaven as they lowered the coffin into the ground.

They dug Fernando Malevento up, his protectors, and they handed him a white silk handkerchief. "For Tommy California," they told him in the graveyard, "for when you get to New York." Fernando Malevento made a fist around the handkerchief with his left hand.

They put him in the hold of a ship going to New York, sealed in a crate with food and water. Men he didn't know opened the crate in a warehouse near the East River. When Fernando Malevento came out into the daylight, he was blind. He wouldn't speak until he could see, and he wouldn't let go of the white silk handkerchief until he had put it into Tommy California's hand.

Fernando Malevento was trained in the old ways, but he didn't look back. He called himself Nicky in the new country and the neighborhood called him Mole because he had lived under the earth. He got rid of everybody Tommy California didn't like, and then he got rid of Tommy California. The body was never found. Father Giannini sent the soul of the dead man up to heaven and they buried an empty box. There was a very large floral arrangement from Nicky Malevento. AMICO was written across it in red-and-gold paper letters.

The enemies of Nicky Mole said he was afraid of the dark. "It's only natural," they said. "Think of the coffin, the crate, dark like death." But it wasn't true. Nicky Mole's story began long before he was sealed in a crate in the hold of a ship. He was from Naples, from the *bassi*, those windowless ground floors where it was always dark. He had spent his childhood there, and many hours under the bed where his mother took her lovers. The dark comforted him. Nicky Mole had no fears and no weaknesses . . . until Carolina Magro.

Joey Dee knew he couldn't sneak around forever. He couldn't show he was afraid. He had to keep his face. The neighborhood never forgot. You couldn't go far enough away. They talked about you after you were dead.

On Monday he stayed in bed until his father left and then he went down. It was early, and outside Nicky Mole's cafe Benny Scar was listening to some guy's story about why his vig was late, how he'd double up next week.

The storefront was streaked with dust and the lettering on the windows was peeling. No one remembered what had been printed on the windows. When Nicky Mole took over he left the windows the way they were. Everyone knew where he was and who he was. He didn't have to advertise.

Benny Scar saw Joey Dee and chased the guy he was talking to. Benny Scar waited for Joey Dee to get close. He waited for him to speak first.

"Is Nicky around?" Joey Dee said.

"He just left," Benny Scar told him. "You just missed him. Try later, sometime this afternoon." Benny Scar smiled.

"Like two, three o'clock?"

"Yeah, that's good. Try then."

Joey Dee walked a few doors up and went into the Allegra Coffee Bar and ordered an espresso, a short one. He spilled most of it. The waitress mopped up the table and kept her eyes down. Joey Dee had gone to school with her but she didn't say hello. All the guys who go to see Benny Scar without the vig must come in here and spill coffee, Joey Dee thought.

He left her a two-dollar tip so she wouldn't think he was one of those bums who owed, and he went to stand by Sammy One-eye's building to wait for Josie Magro.

It was a shit hole of a building, with the toilets in the hall. There were no baths. He wondered how Carolina Magro managed to look the way she did, living in a building like that. Not just clean—everyone was clean, if you didn't count Vito Santero, who didn't know clean from dirty—but done up, always done up, always looking like she was on her way to someplace.

Joey Dee waited for Josie Magro, to tell her it was over and they should stop, but he was thinking about Carolina Magro. He had been thinking about her since Sonny Magro's wake, about her red mouth, about how the gold bracelet looked under her black stocking at Sonny Magro's funeral.

Josie Magro would come down to shop for her mother because Carolina Magro didn't shop. She didn't get up early. "She's got it good," the ladies said. "She would have a hard time, that one, if she had to do things for herself. They love you more," the ladies said, "the worse you are. They want you. Us, we're good. We give it all. What's left to want?"

Josie Magro came down at ten to ten. "What hole did you crawl out of?" she said when she saw Joey Dee. She walked past him. He touched her arm and she turned. She spat on the ground in front of him.

"You're a real lady," Joey Dee said. "Let's get out of here. We'll go uptown. I'll take you for something to eat."

"I gotta shop," she said.

Joey Dee followed her around, to Mario's for meat, to Gracie's for cheese. He followed her up the church steps and inside, where she lit a candle. He held out the dollar for the candle, but she let it drop to the floor. He didn't pick it up.

"I'm sorry about your father, Josie. But you weren't at the wake or the funeral or nothing. What was I supposed to do?" Joey Dee told her this all the way down the church steps.

Near the park, Josie Magro stopped and faced him. "I been looking for you," she said. "You know how many times I come and called for you in the hallway? You're deaf? Your mother can't hear either?"

They were standing on the sidewalk in front of where the ladies sat on park benches with their fat knees apart, their stockings rolled and held with rubber bands. In summer the ladies came out early into the cool of the park. They took up the best benches, under the trees. The sun made them sweat and darkened their skin.

"Let's go, Josie. Let's get out of here." Joey Dee looked over at the ladies on the park benches. "Why you gotta give them something else to say about you?"

"You're not worried about me, Joey. You're worried about you. You don't want nobody to talk about you and me in the same breath. And you know what, Joey? You can drop dead."

The ladies looked and they listened.

"Bitch," Joey Dee said. He said it low. "Crazy bitch, you're crazy, you know that?" He kicked the fire hydrant and walked away. She always made a scene, Josie. She always did that. She didn't care who saw what. She knew he hated commotions. She knew that.

He went uptown alone and saw a movie. He thought about Josie Magro. He imagined her knocked up, coming to tell him, crying . . . It made him feel good to think of Josie Magro crying to him, but he knew she never would. She'd never even tell him if she got knocked up. She'd do something, her and her whore mother. Joey Dee talked to himself in the dark of the Loew's theater, in the top balcony. He saw Carolina Magro on the big screen. She wore a black dress and a gold bracelet under one silk stocking.

Joey Dee passed by Nicky Mole's cafe at three. The door was partly open. Inside, the men drank coffee; they played pinochle. Sometimes there was swag in the back, and if Nicky Mole was out, Fat Frankie would sell it to everyone who passed. Nicky Mole didn't like Fat Frankie doing this, so Fat Frankie did it when he wasn't around. As long as Fat Frankie gave Nicky Mole that respect and kicked back some of the action, he let it go by.

If Fat Frankie had something good, the whole neighborhood had it three days later. If it was garbage, you had to buy it anyway. What could you do? Joey Dee had bought Chinese vases and picnic hampers. He had bought writing paper and rubber boots and a lamp with a picture of a horse on it. He had never wanted anything he bought from Fat Frankie in the back of Nicky Mole's cafe.

Joey Dee went inside. There was a pinochle game going on in one corner. Jumbo was behind the bar steaming milk.

"Nicky here?" Joey Dee said to no one in particular. The card players didn't look up. No one answered.

Jumbo saw it was Joey Dee. "He just left," he told him.

"Come by later," someone at the pinochle table said.

"Yeah, I will. Thanks."

Joey Dee didn't know how much longer he could take this. The light outside hurt his eyes. He walked to the corner, hands in his pocket. When he passed the park, he called hello to each of the ladies by name to take his mind off things.

Carolina Magro was just getting up. Josie had left coffee and rolls from Canapa's. Carolina loved Josie unconditionally, the way her mother had loved her.

Carolina's mother said that Fate had put its fat thumb in her neck and crushed her like a beetle, except for Carolina. God had smiled on her when he gave her Carolina.

Carolina Magro poured her coffee and wondered what would be. She tried hard to control her destiny, to keep Fate's fat thumb away. She thought about Sonny Magro and how he had looked that Sunday morning before nine o'clock Mass, broken like that, his blood in the street.

Carolina never went to Mass, but the commotion outside that morning had woken her up, had pulled her to the window. She had gone downstairs in her slippers and a silk robe, the kind of robe women wore in the movies, and she had stood near the body, near the feet. The blood had stained the bottom of the robe.

The ladies had watched for her to shout, to fall across the body of her husband, to put her eyes to heaven and swear revenge. Carolina had smoothed back her hair. She had looked at the ladies, at their faces under the big hats, and had pulled her robe tightly against her legs and walked back into the building. It was quiet then. They could hear the heels of her slippers on the stairs.

*   *   *

The gossip when Sonny Magro took out Carolina was that she was Tommy California's girl, but Sonny Magro asked her to marry him anyway and she said yes.

This had made the mother happy. The ladies couldn't whisper anymore, the mother told Carolina. Those *stregas* would finally know she had raised a good daughter. The mother held Carolina's head in her hands and kissed her forehead. Sonny Magro is a good catch, she had whispered.

The mother wore blue at the wedding. Donna Vecchio wore rose. She had had first pick.

Carolina bought the mother's dress at Saks. The dress came from France and there were matching shoes. The money for the mother's dress and shoes came from Tommy California, who disappeared not long after the wedding. Not even the ladies could make a connection between the events.

The mother took Carolina aside at the wedding. "Bury me in this dress," she told her, "and these shoes, too."

Carolina promised. She had made the mother happy with this marriage, but she realized that first night, when Sonny Magro called her into the kitchen, that the price she had paid was too high.

Sonny Magro sat in the kitchen that first night and held the *busta*, the white satin wedding bag stuffed with envelopes. He emptied it onto the table. He wanted to open the envelopes before anything else, he told Carolina. He wanted her to write down the names of who had given and how much. His mother would ask for the list, he said. She would want to know.

Sonny Magro had opened the envelopes and Carolina had written the names down one side of a piece of paper, the amounts down the other. She didn't tell him about the ten one-hundred-dollar bills from Tommy California. She had torn the hem of her wedding dress and put them inside. A good-bye gift, Tommy California had said. She wondered later if he had known he was leaving for good.

There had been no honeymoon. Sonny Magro didn't want one. His brother had gone all the way to Atlantic City, he told her, and it had rained. All that money for nothing. They had to be serious now. They had to be careful. They were married.

Carolina knew that first night that she had made a terrible mistake.

Sonny Magro called her careless. He had never heard of a woman like her, he said. His mother could manage on nothing. Over and over, he told her this. He took the household money away from her. She couldn't manage it, he said.

Carolina embarrassed him. She had her hair done and didn't give Sammy One-eye the rent. She took cabs uptown and ate lunch in outdoor cafes. People had seen her. People had told him.

So Sonny Magro gave her just so much, and on Fridays he payed the shopkeepers for the week. They showed him his account in their black-and-white notebooks. When he came home from the post office at four, he started dinner.

Sonny Magro had a wife who wouldn't cook and couldn't manage. So what if she was beautiful? his mother had told him. What good was it to have a wife that other men wanted?

As for Carolina Magro, she fancied things, so she took the job cleaning Nicky Mole's office. The job was easy, the pay was good. Sonny Magro was too tight with a buck. These were her reasons. She didn't think about consequences. She was instinctive and easily bored.

Carolina Magro poured more coffee. The sun was in the kitchen, the windows coated with dust. She couldn't keep house, Sonny Magro had told her. Poor Sonny Magro, she thought, stirring sugar into her coffee. He had been right about some things.

She didn't like to remember him in the street. She had worried about Josie. She had felt angry and guilty and relieved that morning when she stood by his body in the street, but when she saw him laid out at Gambino's Funeral Parlor, she had felt nothing.

She had walked into the funeral parlor alone that first night he was laid out. She had stood near the coffin and thought that Sonny Magro would die all over again if he knew what his suit cost.

She felt the ladies watch her. She felt her importance in their lives. Of course, there were others: Cettina had run away with the priest. Maria Vizzini's uncle had given her a baby with two heads. But Carolina had been special from her beginnings.

Carolina leaned back, tipped her chair against the wall. She knew nothing of the future, but she knew this: He would get in touch with her before long. She wasn't afraid. Carolina had never been afraid of anything.

Fernando ("Nicky Mole") Malevento did not need women. He could have them if he wanted, but he didn't. From when he was a young man, in the *bassi* of Naples, he didn't. What he wanted was money and the power that went with it.

His mother, her beauty having betrayed her years ago, had turned her passion to the church. When Fernando didn't court the local girls, she decided he should be a man of God. She told her son she had seen him in a dream, in the brown robe of the Franciscan. She went to the *strega* to fulfill the dream. She prayed and made novenas to Santa Rosalina. She went without meals.

Fernando Malevento killed his first man at seventeen.

His mother never forgave him or Santa Rosalina for disappointing her. The statue of Santa Rosalina she threw in the local well. When she saw her son in the street, she spat on the ground in front of him.

Fernando Malevento bought her things she didn't want and wouldn't use. He said he would make her a *signora*. Water would run from a tap in her house. A woman would wash her clothes and cook her food.

"You know what God thinks of money," she told him. "Look who he gives it to." She said if he came to her wake she would get up and leave.

From America, Nicky Mole sent her packages that always came back, so he sent a courier with money for her, to put it in her hands. He gave the courier a packet stuffed with American dollars, and told him where and to whom it should be delivered. He did not say the woman was his mother.

The courier came back with the packet. He was afraid to tell Nicky Mole what had happened. "She wouldn't take it," the courier said. "When she heard it was from America, she refused. I tried for three days. I rented a room next to hers in the *bassi*. She cursed me in a dialect I could not understand."

Nicky Mole sent the courier back. But this time he carried a sealed message that said: Mama, if this young boy returns with the packet meant for you, his blood is on your hands.

She took the packet. Nicky Mole wasn't so sure she would. He was relieved to find out she had. She had taken the packet stuffed with American dollars and she had given the money to the people in the *bassi*, her neighbors, who took it to the black market.

They praised Don Malevento from New York. They promised him their prayers. They said she was a lucky woman to have such a son who had done so well and remembered her from so far away.

Nicky Mole was too busy for women and the chaos they caused. He saw the men around him with wives and children and mistresses. It weakened them, he thought. It exposed them.

It was enough for Nicky Mole to have his hand kissed, to have eyes lowered in his presence, to be spoken about in reverent whispers. There was power and there was money. Sexuality, he knew, was obsessive, and he refused it.

But Carolina Magro made Nicky Mole forget what he knew. He said later that she had hexed him. He smiled when he said this, but secretly he believed she had put a spell on him, that he had ingested her hair, her menstrual blood. There was no other way he could account for his feelings.

Nicky Mole needed someone to clean his office. It was a little job for big pay. Nicky Mole was a fair and generous man. He expected one of the neighborhood widows to get the job, one of the old women with thick veins at her ankles. He left it up to Benny Scar and forgot about it.

Benny Scar had different ideas. He had an eye for the women, and when Carolina Magro asked about the job, she had no competition.

Carolina Magro worked for three months before Nicky Mole saw her. She had left her ring in the office. She had taken it off at the sink and forgotten it.

Nicky Mole was in the office when she came to get it. He didn't know who she was. He thought she was cheap-looking. Her mouth was too red and her hair was too black. A *strega*, he thought.

But after that time, he would look for her. He would come to the office when he knew she was there. He would watch her. She would paint her mouth in the mirror, smooth her eyebrows with a finger.

She never cleaned. The ashtrays were emptied but never washed. The floor was grimy. He thought that if he could see her on her knees, her knuckles white from the effort of wringing out a rag, he would not want her anymore, so he told her to wash the floor.

Carolina Magro wouldn't. She knew where she stood. She had him in her underpants, the mother would have said.

"I should let you go," he told her. "You get paid for nothing."

Carolina put on her hat and coat and didn't come back for three days. Nicky Mole came every afternoon to wait for her. He could not believe her character, that she had no fear, no respect. Brave men, important men, kissed his hand. This woman took his money for nothing.

She was married, he found out. She had a child. He didn't like any of this, but he was caught. He was in her underpants.

She came at the end of the week. For her pay, she said.

"I don't pay the help," he told her. "I don't deal with maids."

"I won't be back." Her mouth was very red.

"Come tomorrow," he said.

She shrugged.

Carolina Magro came the next day. Her mouth was particularly red and her hair particularly black. Nicky Mole handed her an envelope. Inside were hundred-dollar bills and a pearl necklace with a diamond clasp.

Carolina Magro took out the bills. "This is too much," she told him. She held up the pearls. "And what do I do with these?"

"Wear them for me," he said.

Carolina put on the pearls and took off everything else.

FOUR

The neighborhood had a stickball game in Sonny Magro's memory. Joey Dee's father was there. All the working guys were there. Joey Dee didn't call them pants pressers where his father could hear. Joey Dee was a tough guy but he knew his limits.

The men played the game in the street where they had played as boys, the end of Thompson Street, where the trucks moved in and out of the warehouse on the corner. The women put pillows under their elbows and leaned out of windows. People brought folding chairs and lunch.

Carolina Magro didn't come but Josie Magro did. The ladies asked after her mother. To be polite, they said.

"She can't come down," Josie told them. When she smiled at the ladies, she showed all her teeth.

"Like a terrier," the ladies said. They told the stories about her when she walked away.

"A wife can make you, a wife can break you," the men said to each other about Sonny Magro. There was a feeling that Carolina Magro was responsible for Sonny Magro's fate, but not even the ladies could say exactly how.

Joey Dee came to the stickball game alone. He had things on his mind. Mikey Bats and Carmine were there, and he waved when he saw them. He caught hold of Josie Magro's arm between innings and she didn't pull away.

"Meet me later?" he said, and Josie Magro nodded.

Joey Dee didn't think anyone had seen them, but when he went over to where his mother sat and asked for a sandwich, she narrowed her eyes. "You gonna leave that girl alone?" she said low so no one else could hear. She didn't hand the sandwich up to him. She held it near her lap, so Joey Dee had to bend down, had to get close to her. "I never bother you," she said.

"Then don't start now," he told her. He unwrapped the sandwich and put the wax paper in her lap. She folded it into a neat square. She pressed out the wrinkles and put it back into her bag.

Father Giannini gave a eulogy at the end of the game. He said what he always said, but then Sonny Magro's buddies got up, one by one, and told stories about him—men who worked with him at the post office, men he went to school with. At the end, when the last man had spoken, the sky covered over with fat white clouds.

"Sonny Magro sent them," the ladies told each other, to let them all know he was in heaven like Father Giannini said.

Joey Dee's mother repeated this at supper. She loved the idea of Sonny Magro in heaven. It was not important why he had died or who had killed him. He was up there in the fat white clouds.

Joey Dee said he was going down, going out, and didn't answer when his mother asked him what time he was coming home. He went down the steps two at a time and into the streets, which were only now cooling off.

Joey Dee met Josie and he didn't tell her it was over. They

started up where they had left off. He took a room on Thirty-third Street near Macy's and they spent the night. There wasn't another girl in the neighborhood who would do this. Good girls didn't do this. They might, if they were engaged, or almost engaged, maybe, but never in a hotel.

Joey Dee had blessed his good luck that first time he asked Josie Magro to go there with him, and she had said yes, but after, when he lay with her, the blinds shut tight against the outside, he thought what his mother would have thought, what the ladies would have thought.

"Her mother's daughter," they would say. "Make no mistake. It's in the blood."

It bothered Joey Dee that Josie Magro had been so easy. When he got mad at her, he would accuse her of going with anybody and everybody. He would say she went with Mikey Bats and Carmine behind his back, that she took Vito in the alley, near the ashcans, and put it in her mouth.

"And Tommy California, him too," Joey Dee would say.

"You're so stupid. Tommy California's fucking dead." Josie Magro would tell him. "He was dead before I was born."

"That's right, I get mixed up," Joey Dee said. "It was your mother fucked Tommy California."

Josie Magro would come at him when he said these things. If they were in the hotel, she would break something and he would have to pay for it. She would break a mirror, a lamp. She broke a window once and the manager called the cops. It cost Joey Dee fifty dollars that time, twenty-five for the window and twenty-five for the cops.

Joey Dee called her crazy, but he never went with another girl. She was there for him, even after he would walk past her on Sullivan Street like she was nobody.

She would look at him when he would do this and silently form her mouth around vulgar words. Later, alone with her in the room on Thirty-third Street, he would say he was sorry. Josie Magro took things as they came. Joey Dee never knew how she really felt.

*   *   *

Joey Dee got home the next day in time for supper, smelling of Josie Magro. At the table his father told him he had gotten him a job.

"A job?" Joey Dee said.

"You start tomorrow."

"Tomorrow? I can't. I can't tomorrow."

"Oh yeah? Why not, wise guy? What's so special about tomorrow?"

"Don't I need some kind of clothes? You know I got no work clothes," Joey Dee said.

"Patsy Monk said you should bring an overcoat and galoshes. That's all you need."

"It's August," Joey Dee said.

"Eat," his mother said. "Finish your food. How can you work if you don't eat?"

"Eat? I can't eat. He's sitting here telling me I got a job tomorrow, I need an overcoat and galoshes in August, and you expect me to eat?" Joey Dee pushed back his chair and stood up. "I'm going down," he said.

"You should get some sleep," his father said. "Patsy's picking you up at four."

"Four? Four what? In the morning?"

"Yeah," his father said. His mother cleared the dishes. She shook her head at the food Joey Dee had left on his plate.

At four the next morning Joey Dee was outside his building on Spring Street with his winter coat over his arm, holding his galoshes. Patsy Monk pulled up smiling and honked the horn.

Joey Dee was glad it was four in the morning. There wasn't much chance of anyone seeing him standing there, holding his winter coat and galoshes, getting into a car with Patsy Monk.

Joey Dee was usually just getting home at four, moving fast to beat the light coming up. Dracula, his father called him.

"This is real nice of you, Patsy, getting me this job."

"It's nothing," Patsy Monk said. "Just put your stuff back there with mine." Joey Dee saw Patsy's coat and galoshes in the backseat and felt sick. He had hoped his father had made up the part about the coat and galoshes just to scare him, to get even, but there they were. He threw his coat and boots on top of Patsy Monk's and got in the car.

"Your father was real happy about this. 'I owe you, Patsy,' he said to me. It's a good job, you know. Pension, a week off after two years. It's a little far, but I'll take you, no problem. I could use the company. It's a long drive."

Patsy Monk talked the whole way up. He told Joey Dee about his wife's hot flashes, about her hysterectomy, about her hemorrhoids. It was almost five-thirty before Patsy Monk pulled into a fenced parking lot somewhere in the asshole of the Bronx, where men were standing outside their cars buttoning up overcoats and pulling on rubber boots. Some of the men had on wool hats and gloves without fingers. It was ninety degrees.

Joey Dee wished his father cancer. He took it back. Patsy Monk told him to hurry up, that he couldn't be late the first day. Patsy Monk took Joey Dee inside. The warehouse was a huge freezer filled with chickens hanging on hooks from conveyor belts. There were two sections.

On one side men pinned fresh-killed chickens, wet and steaming, onto the rotating hooks. On the other side they took frozen chickens off the hooks and loaded them into boxes.

The men went back and forth from the outside, unloading fresh chickens and loading the frozen ones. They pushed hand trucks full of chickens back and forth from the parking lot to the freezer.

"Stay with me," Patsy Monk told Joey Dee, "until you get the hang of it."

It was freezing inside the warehouse. The sweat from push-

ing the hand trucks formed ice on the men's eyebrows.
Threads of ice hung from their noses. The ice melted when
they pushed the carts back outside into the August heat, and
ran down their faces. Joey Dee wished his father cancer, the
worst kind. He spent the morning deciding what the worst
kind was.

A whistle blew at eleven-thirty. "Lunch break," Patsy
Monk said. They sat in the parking lot in the sun. Joey Dee's
mother had sent two sandwiches. They were both eggplant.
He wished they were poisoned.

At the last whistle, Joey Dee took off his galoshes and overcoat and put them in the trash bin. Patsy Monk got frantic.
"What are you doing? You crazy?" he said.

"They smell of chicken," Joey Dee told him.

"So, whatta you expect? Perfume? You need them clothes
for tomorrow."

"I'm not coming tomorrow," Joey Dee said.

"I don't understand," Patsy Monk said. "It's a good job.
You think jobs like this grow on trees? What's the matter with
you?"

Joey Dee lit a cigarette and threw the match out the window. "Patsy, please. Let's get back."

"OK, fine."

Patsy Monk talked the whole way down. When he pulled
up in front of Joey Dee's building, it was six o'clock. "I'll pick
you up tomorrow," he said.

"Don't pick me up tomorrow, Patsy. I ain't going."

"You're father'll kill you, you blow this job."

"Patsy," Joey Dee said, "I'd rather be dead."

Joey Dee kept stopping by Nicky Mole's cafe, but Nicky
Mole was never there. They always told him to come back
that afternoon, tomorrow, Wednesday. They told him not to
forget. Joey Dee didn't forget, but he had other things on his
mind, too. He was trying to avoid his father.

After the chicken factory, he had stopped going home. He

was staying across the hall with his Aunt Julia. She had boy-friends who visited at odd hours. This made Joey Dee's father crazy. He said he had a whore for a sister and a bum for a son. The two of them would kill him someday, he said, if he didn't kill them first.

This morning Joey Dee went to Rocky's for a haircut because Aunt Julia was expecting a friend. There were three guys ahead of him at Rocky's and Joey Dee sat down to wait. Sammy One-eye was in the chair getting a shave. He was leaning back in the chair with his eyes closed.

Rocky finished the left side of Sammy One-eye's face, the side with the eye, and was starting on the right when Nicky Mole walked in.

Rocky looked up. The men looked down. Rocky cut Sammy One-eye's face, a very small cut, near his ear. Nicky Mole made a movement with his hand, a very small movement. The men waiting stood up.

Rocky gave Sammy One-eye a cotton ball dipped in antiseptic and whispered for him to get out of the chair. He told him to press on the cotton ball to stop the bleeding. The men went outside to wait, to stand with their backs to the window. Sammy One-eye followed, his face half covered in shaving foam, holding the cotton ball red with the blood from the very small cut near his ear. Joey Dee stood outside with the men. No one spoke. Joey Dee thought about Las Vegas and the desert.

Inside, Rocky heated the towels. Nicky Mole sat in the barber chair. Benny Scar and Fat Frankie came in and talked to Nicky Mole while Rocky shaved him. If they said something Nicky Mole didn't like, he would want to hit them, so they never stood too near. They knew he couldn't move quickly because of the hot towels and the foam and Rocky with that straight razor in his hand.

Rocky's arthritis would act up when Nicky Mole came into the barbershop. It was his nerves, Rocky said. His bones would hurt like it was raining. His head would start to pound. Rocky was afraid he would hear something he wasn't supposed to hear, that Nicky Mole would slip, make a mistake, and then Rocky would never get to retire in Florida.

When Nicky Mole was shaved and he had heard what Benny Scar and Fat Frankie had to say, he got up and walked out. Benny Scar put money in Rocky's hand. The men, he said, pointing through the window, their haircuts, their shaves, were on Nicky. Rocky should tell them that.

Outside, Nicky Mole thanked the men for waiting. He mentioned to Sammy One-eye that he was bleeding from a cut near his ear.

Benny Scar and Fat Frankie came out of the barbershop and were about to follow Nicky Mole up the street when Benny Scar spotted Joey Dee. He motioned to Fat Frankie not to wait and went over to where Joey Dee was standing.

"Hey," he said. "Weren't you supposed to come by and see Nicky? Didn't I tell you that?"

"I came by," Joey Dee said.

"Did you see him?"

"No . . . he . . ."

"Then it don't count. Nicky wants to see you. He don't like to wait. It don't show no respect. You know about respect, don't you?" Benny Scar put one hand on Joey Dee's shoulder. He patted his face with the other. "Come around," he said. "It don't look good, you wait too long."

Joey Dee went to Nicky Mole's cafe that afternoon. Nicky Mole, Benny Scar, Fat Frankie, and Jumbo were sitting at a table in the corner. The cards were out.

Nicky Mole hit Fat Frankie on the side of his head with the fan of cards he held in his hand. "Stupid," he said. "Why are you so stupid? How could you play that card? Can't you remember nothing, for Chrissakes?" He looked up and saw Joey Dee in the doorway. "You play pinochle, kid?" he said to him.

Joey Dee put his palms out in front of him. He shrugged and opened his mouth to answer.

"Sit down," Nicky Mole said. "Give him your cards," he told Fat Frankie. "I can't take it no more, the way you play."

Fat Frankie got up. Nicky Mole ordered coffee. Jumbo got up. "Sit down," Nicky Mole said. "You're playing cards." He waved a hand at Fat Frankie. "You make the coffee."

Jumbo's eyes bulged. Jumbo hated pinochle. He was bad at it. The regular guy was sick and Nicky Mole put Jumbo in the game because he wanted to play. Jumbo was just there to make the coffee, answer the pay phone in the closet. He was out of work, and Benny Scar had gotten him the job because Jumbo was married to Benny Scar's wife's first cousin. He was not as grateful for the opportunity as Benny thought he should be. He whispered to Joey Dee to play good but not to win.

"What the hell does that mean?" Joey Dee whispered back. He felt the sweat starting under his collar, his throat closing. A sit-down with Nicky Mole was bad, but a pinochle game was worse. Nicky Mole was fanatical about pinochle. He played it every day. He played for money and he was fanatical about money.

Joey Dee picked up his hand. Jumbo went to close the door.

"Not bad for a kid," Nicky Mole said four hours later. "No, Benny? He did good. You hear that, Frankie?" Nicky Mole shouted over to Fat Frankie, who sat in the opposite corner reading the newspaper. "He's just a kid and he plays better than you. How come you can't play good like him?"

Jumbo shifted in his seat. "Can I clear the cups, boss? Make more coffee?"

Nicky Mole waved his hand. "Just get out of here," he said and turned to Joey Dee.

"What's your name?"

"This is Joey De Stefano," Benny Scar said. "I was telling you about him."

"Joey, right, now I remember. He looks like a smart kid. How old are you, kid?"

"Old enough," Joey Dee said. Nicky Mole laughed. Joey Dee didn't know where to put his eyes. His hands were under the table. He thought about a cigarette, but there was no ashtray on the table. He worried about where he would blow the smoke.

"And what do you do?" Nicky Mole said. He looked at Joey Dee as though he were interesting. It seemed to Joey Dee that Nicky Mole didn't blink, that he had no eyelids.

"I work here and there." Joey Dee looked down at Nicky Mole's hands, at the size of them. He wore no rings, but his hands were manicured, the nails painted with clear polish.

"Maybe I can do something for you," Nicky Mole said. He turned to Benny Scar. "Remind me," he said, "to see if there's anything for this kid . . . Joey, right?"

Joey Dee nodded.

"Remind me to find something for Joey."

Nicky Mole stood up. Benny Scar gave Joey Dee the evil eye, the eye to get up and move out of there. Joey Dee pushed back the chair. He forced himself to move slowly. Benny Scar walked him out. He held him under the arm.

"Come back soon," he said and patted Joey Dee on the back.

Joey Dee was out the door and into the street. He wanted to get off Sullivan Street fast. His whole goddamn life was on this block, he thought, the church, the school. It was where he kept his birds, where Josie Magro lived, where Vito Santero moved the ashcans from the sidewalk to the alley, where Sonny Magro was killed. He wished he could get out of here for good. If he could get a bankroll together, enough to get started, he could go to Vegas.

"That fucking Vito," he said aloud. "That fucking retarded moron." They must know, he thought. What was all this bullshit? It had to do with Vito Santero's big mouth and his big ears and his big eyes. He should have stayed in bed that

Sunday morning. He should have stayed in bed his whole life. He should have died when he was born, like his father always said.

Joey Dee's father caught him in the hallway when he came into the building on Spring Street. He was waiting for Joey Dee under the stairs. He smacked him hard. He grabbed his collar in his hands.

"But what's with you?" he said. "It never stops with you? You never know when to stop?"

"What?" Joey Dee said. "What are you talking about? What are you doing hanging around under the stairs?"

"Never mind," his father said. "What were you doing in Nicky Mole's cafe? What's going on with you? You borrowing money? You gambling? Or you just sticking your nose up somebody's ass?"

"Nothing," Joey Dee said. "I swear on your mother, nothing. Jumbo called me in. They needed a fourth for pinochle. That's all. You think I wanted to go in there?"

"Since when do you play pinochle?"

"I can play pinochle."

Joey Dee's father let go of his collar. "Well, stay out of there. And get your stuff out of Aunt Julia's, that other *scucciande*. Your mother wants you home."

"You threw me out."

"Did I ask you a question?"

"No . . . but—"

"Then I'm not looking for no answer."

Joey Dee went up the stairs to the fourth floor. His collar was bent from his father's pulling on it. He was sweaty and wrinkled. He wondered how much longer this day could last.

FIVE

Joey Dee's father said his mother ruined him with her babying, but living with Aunt Julia was no better, so he might as well come home. Joey Dee moved back across the hall. Then everything got quiet and the quiet made Joey Dee nervous.

His father left him alone. The door to Nicky Mole's cafe was always padlocked when he passed, and Josie Magro took afternoons off to meet him in the hotel room on Thirty-third Street. The ladies were silent on the park bench, drops of sweat shining on the dark hair of their upper lips. It was too hot even for August.

Vito Santero moved the ashcans back and forth in front of Sammy One-eye's building, and would start to talk too loud when Joey Dee came by. Sometimes he would cry. Always he would wipe his nose with his sleeve, but Joey Dee managed to stay away.

Carmine had started taking book for Benny Scar and had money to burn, so the three of

them, Joey Dee, Mikey Bats, and Carmine, went to the movies a
lot. They went to shoot pool. They sat in Dirty Waters's ice cream
parlor and ate grilled cheese sandwiches and tuna fish on rye.

Carmine had a car now. He went to Rocky's barbershop on
Wednesdays, when the girl was there, and got a manicure.
He carried his money folded in half in a silver money clip
engraved with his initials. The top bill was a fifty, but Carmine called it "half a yard."

The three of them were taking a ride up the parkway, Joey
Dee, Mikey Bats, and Carmine. They were looking at the river.

"Which river is this?" Mikey Bats said. "I always get mixed
up."

"We're on the East Side, Mikey. This is the East River.
How the hell can you get mixed up?" Carmine took one hand
off the wheel and pushed it against Mikey Bats's head.

"Yeah, but we come from the West Side, so how come
we're on the East Side? Why didn't we go up the West Side?

"I don't know," Carmine said. "We're just taking a ride."

Joey Dee sat in the back. He rolled down the window and
turned his face into the wind. The air outside felt different.
He could smell the river, but it wasn't just that. The air always felt different to Joey Dee when he was away from the
neighborhood. He felt different.

"So what's new, Joey?" Carmine said. "You're always so
quiet. You were never quiet."

"Joey was always quiet," Mikey Bats said. "You're the one
with the big mouth, the big shot with the big mouth."

"What's with you?" Carmine said. "A guy does good, you
begrudge him? I couldn't take it no more, never no money in
my pocket. It's easy what I'm doing. I like the action. I told
you I'd get you in if you want. There's always room." Carmine turned around to face Joey Dee. "You could go down
the docks, Joey. Shit-house Tony is retiring, going to Florida.
I could talk to Benny for you."

"Thanks," Joey Dee said. "Don't do me no favors. My old
man's finally off my back. He'd kill me if I tried to take over
the action down the docks. He works there, remember?"

"Didn't you work there, Joey?" Mikey Bats said. "Didn't he get you a job down there?"

"Yeah, carrying bananas. Don't remind me. What a shit job that was. Tarantulas all over the place."

Carmine looked back at Joey Dee. He had one hand on the wheel, his elbow out the window. "You know, not for nothing, Joey, but Benny's been asking about you. What's going on?"

"What do I know? You're the one's in bed with Benny Scar, not me." Joey Dee looked out the window at the river when he said this.

"What ever happened with the sit-down?"

"Nothing," Joey Dee said. "I told you. I played pinochle with Benny Scar and the Mole."

"You know, not for nothing, Joey, but don't ever let Benny hear you call him Scar. He's sensitive about it. Nicky, too . . . They don't like them names."

"Oh, yeah, right, Carmine. Thanks for the tip."

Carmine never said "Nicky Mole" or "Benny Scar." He said "Nicky" and he said "Benny." When Carmine brought the bets he had collected to Benny Scar, he would stand outside the cafe longer than he had to. He would ask Benny Scar how he felt. Benny Scar could go on for a long time about how he felt, how his ears rang and how he couldn't sleep. Carmine liked to stand outside the cafe on Sullivan Street. He liked the neighborhood to see him out there. If one of the ladies passed, he'd touch the brim of his hat the way Nicky Mole would. Carmine wore a Borsalino, like Nicky Mole, and he wore it pulled low to one side, like Nicky Mole.

"I can't figure it," Carmine said to Joey Dee after a long pause. "That ain't like Nicky to let things go."

Joey Dee didn't answer. Carmine lit a cigarette. Mikey Bats played with the radio. Joey Dee rolled down the window as far as it would go and put his face out.

The next time Joey Dee got the word, it was not from Benny Scar. Carmine came to call for him, stood at the foot

of the stairs in the hallway and yelled up his name. Joey Dee
was still in bed, in the folding *brande* his mother opened up
for him every night in the kitchen.

His father looked over from the table where he was sitting.
"Get up," he said.

"Let him sleep," Joey Dee's mother said.

"Why?"

"It's Saturday."

"It's always Saturday for him. He don't work." Joey Dee's
father went over and shook him. He pulled his hair. "One of
your bum friends is calling for you," he said. "Get up."

Joey Dee covered his head with his pillow. His mother
went out into the hall and called downstairs for Carmine to
come up. When he did, Joey Dee's father looked him over.

"Fancy, ain't we?" he said. "What are you doing these days?"

Carmine shrugged. He thanked Joey Dee's mother when
she poured him coffee. "You want eggs?" she said. "I can
make you eggs."

"No, thanks."

"You want toast?"

"No, no thank you."

"I got panettone. I can put it in the oven . . ."

"No, really . . . I—"

"For Chrissakes, Ma, he don't want nothing." Joey Dee got
out of bed.

"Maybe he's shy. I'm only asking."

"So what are you doing with yourself?" Joey Dee's father
said to Carmine.

"Oh, things here and there, you know." Carmine cracked
his knuckles.

"Yeah, I know." He turned to Joey Dee, who was up at the
sink washing. "And where are you going?" he said.

"I don't know . . . out."

"When are you going to get a job?"

"Leave him alone," Joey Dee's mother said. "He's only a
kid. He's got no mouths to feed."

"No, only me, I got mouths to feed." Joey Dee's father got up from the table. "Take it easy," he said to Carmine.

Joey Dee buttoned up his shirt. His mother put a line of toothpaste on his toothbrush and handed it to him. She poured his coffee and held it out for him. "Why don't you sit down, eat something. I got panettone. I can—"

"Ma, please, I gotta go. I don't want nothing." Joey Dee took the coffee. He grabbed hold of her and kissed her near her mouth. She put her hand through his hair and then she pushed him away. Carmine said good-bye, and the two of them left.

On the way downstairs, Joey Dee smoothed his hair with both hands. He hated rushing, especially when he was getting dressed. "What's up, Carmine? What are you doing around so early?"

"Early? It's eleven o'clock."

"Since when isn't eleven o'clock early, Carmine? What's going on?"

"Nothing, I thought we'd hang out."

"Where we gonna hang out eleven o'clock in the morning?"

"Breakfast? Let me take you to breakfast."

"Great, where?"

"Your choice."

"Ratner's?"

When they got to Ratner's they sat down in one of the booths by the window and ordered eggs. Then Carmine leaned over the table and told Joey Dee that Nicky Mole wanted to see him, wanted him to stop by the cafe. "You should make it soon," Carmine said.

"And how come you're telling me this, Carmine? You Nicky Mole's messenger boy now?"

"Hey, listen, Joey. We're friends. I thought I was doing you a favor. You want Benny looking for you again? What's the matter with you? I'm trying to help you out."

"Yeah," Joey Dee said. "Then maybe you can tell me why the hell Nicky Mole wants to see me. Can you tell me that?"

Carmine shook his head. "What do I know, Joey? Who am

I, God? I can read Nicky's mind? If I knew I'd tell you."
Carmine leaned back in the booth. "I can tell you one thing,
though."

"What?"

"Don't wear a tie."

"A tie? What are you talking about, Carmine? For
Chrissakes . . ."

"Fine, don't listen, but the last guy wore a tie to a sit-down
with Nicky got strangled with it."

"C'mon, Carmine, please . . ."

"It's true. I swear. My sister should marry Vito Santero."

"You got no sister."

"So what? Just listen, will you? You know how no one fol-
lows Nicky with their eyes? Everyone kind of looks down?
Well, that's what this guy was doing, looking down, and
Nicky walks over in front of him and grabs his tie. He wraps
it around that big hand of his and gives one twist. That was
it. Dead in the chair."

Joey Dee started to laugh. He laughed until he had tears in
eyes. He laughed so hard the waiter came over to see if something was wrong with the eggs.

Joey Dee passed by Nicky Mole's cafe the next afternoon.
The door was shut, but the padlock hung open. Joey Dee
pushed the door open and went inside without knocking.
Benny Scar and Fat Frankie were at a table in the front.
Jumbo was behind the espresso machine.

"Sit down, kid," Benny Scar said. "You want coffee?" He
motioned to Jumbo without waiting for Joey Dee to answer.

Joey Dee sat down and Nicky Mole came through the curtain separating the back room from the cafe. Jumbo brought
the coffee and Benny Scar told him to get lost. He told him to
take a walk around the block.

"Nice to see you again, kid," Nicky Mole said. "Sugar?"
Joey Dee didn't take sugar, but he put two spoonfuls in his
cup. He needed a place to put his hands and his eyes.

Nicky Mole took out a pack of cigarettes and tapped it on the edge of the table. He looked at Joey Dee while he took one out and lit it. "Maybe you could do something for me," Nicky Mole said to Joey Dee. He blew out a steam of smoke. "You seem like a smart kid. I need somebody like you right now. You think you could help me out?"

Joey Dee stirred his coffee. The spoon rang against the inside of the cup. It sounded to Joey Dee like the church bells at a funeral Mass. "Sure," he said. Joey Dee knew the correct answer was "anything," but he couldn't say it. He hoped it wouldn't be "anything." He hoped it would be nothing, like "take my car to be washed," or "drive me uptown."

Nicky Mole picked up his coffee cup and held it near his mouth. "I need someone," he said, "to take a package to the Magro widow. You know who I mean? Her husband was killed a couple of weeks back?"

"On Sunday," Fat Frankie said.

"Shut up," Nicky Mole told him. Nicky Mole drank his coffee. He made a noise with his lips and looked at Joey Dee over the rim of the cup, which was small and disappeared in his big hand. "I'd send one of the boys," he said, "but they're so ugly . . . look at them faces." Nicky Mole pointed at Benny Scar and Fat Frankie. "If I sent these jabonies around to Sullivan Street, the whole neighborhood would be talking. That poor woman's had enough trouble, don't you think?"

Joey Dee nodded.

"Good," Nicky Mole said. He gestured to Fat Frankie, who got up and went behind the curtain into the back. He brought out a letter-sized brown envelope and gave it to Nicky Mole, who handed it to Joey Dee. "Take this," he said, "and when you get a chance you bring it over to her. She's in Sammy One-eye's building, across from the church, apartment five B." Nicky Mole smiled.

Joey Dee took the envelope and said he would bring it. He said he would do it now.

"I knew you were a smart kid," Nicky Mole said. He touched Joey Dee's cheek. Joey Dee remembered Carmine's story, about the guy Nicky Mole strangled with his own tie. Sitting across from Nicky Mole, it didn't seem so funny.

Joey Dee left with the envelope inside his shirt. He knew Josie Magro would be at work, so he decided he would do it now, bring Carolina Magro the envelope now and get it over with.

He got to Sammy One-eye's building across from the church and was going up the stairs when Vito Santero came out of the alley.

"Joey," he said, "Joey, Joey."

"Not now, Vito, I got things to do."

"Where you going, Joey? In the building? You going in the building? Where, Joey, where?"

"Vito, wait for me, OK, I'll be right down. Just wait for me, and shut up. Can you shut up for five minutes?"

Vito sat on the stoop and picked at the threads on his coat sleeves. Joey Dee went in the building and up to apartment 5B.

Carolina Magro was in a robe when she opened the door. It was the robe she was wearing when she came out into the street the Sunday Sonny Magro died. Joey Dee took the envelope out of his shirt. He held it out to her.

"Come in," Carolina Magro said.

"No," Joey Dee told her. "I just gotta give you this."

"What is it?" she said.

Joey Dee shrugged. He didn't want to talk to her. He wanted her to take the package and he wanted to get out of there. He wanted her robe to open so he could see her legs, and the gold bracelet on her left ankle. He wanted the sweat under his collar to stop. "He asked me to bring it to you," Joey Dee said. He felt like a kid when he said this. Wasn't that what Nicky Mole called him, a kid?

"Come inside, or I'm going to shut the door." Carolina Magro said. Joey Dee stepped inside, into the kitchen, and Carolina Magro faced him. "Now," she said, "who is 'he'? You just go around knocking on doors? What's in that envelope?"

"Listen," Joey Dee said. He was getting mad. "I don't know what's in it, but it's yours, so why don't you just take it and let me get out of here?"

"Open it."

Joey Dee put his thumb in the corner of the envelope and tore it open. The envelope was filled with money, old bills, tens, twenties, fifties, hundreds. Some of them fell on the floor.

"You want coffee?" Carolina Magro said. Her robe opened the way he had hoped. He could see the gold bracelet on her left ankle. He could see almost her whole leg. Carolina Magro pushed a chair away from the table. "Sit down," she told him. Her mouth was very red.

Joey Dee picked up the bills that had fallen to the floor, and he put them on the table. "I gotta go," he said. "Some other time." He could hear Vito calling him in the hallway, his name echoing in the stairwell.

Joey Dee turned and walked out. He didn't shut the door. He didn't go down the stairs but up to the roof and down the fire escape. He did this to avoid Vito Santero. He tore a hole in his good pants. He crossed through the back alleys and came out on Thompson Street. Joey Dee put a finger in the hole in his pants and he thought about Las Vegas.

Joey Dee went looking for Mikey Bats and Carmine, to see if they wanted to hang out, maybe fool around with the girls from the commercial high school on MacDougal Street who stayed around when school broke, waiting out their time to be sixteen, to quit school, to work in the sub-basement of the Metropolitan Life Insurance Company. The girls from the commercial high school let cigarettes dangle from their bottom lips and bleached their hair with peroxide until the ends were burnt orange.

But when Joey Dee got there, the girls had already left, had walked west to the tenements near the river where they lived. Carmine was there, though, and he was talking to Josie Magro. She was leaning against the ironwork fence in front of the school, and Carmine was standing in front of her, holding on to the fence with one hand. Josie Magro was leaning back, her hands behind her. She stood with her leg bent, her foot against the fence, looking at Carmine.

Joey Dee wasn't used to what he felt when he saw them. He thought about unhooking Carmine's fingers from the iron-work fence and knocking him into the street. He thought about walking past them like they weren't there and about getting Josie Magro later. "You looked cozy," he would say. "You looked like you didn't want no interruptions."

And Carmine? He would tell him off, too. "What were you doing with Josie Magro?" Joey Dee would say. "You said she was crazy. What were you doing talking to a crazy broad like Josie Magro?"

But instead of doing this, he walked over to them, taking his time. He stood there and looked at the two of them until Carmine turned around and saw him. Carmine kept his hand on the ironwork fence. He stood as near to Josie Magro as he had before he saw Joey Dee, but then, Carmine didn't know. He didn't know Joey Dee took Josie Magro to the hotel on Thirty-third Street near Macy's. Joey Dee had never wanted anyone to know that he went with Josie Magro.

Josie Magro looked at him as if to say this, as if to say that since no one knew she was his, maybe she wasn't, and he could drop dead. Joey Dee could hear her voice in his head, telling him to drop dead.

Josie Magro wouldn't understand that he didn't want anyone to know because he didn't want to spoil it, to see the ladies whispering on the park bench, to hear the neighborhood gossip, to marry her in the church and have Father Giannini say the Mass while all of them put their heads together in the back pews. Josie Magro wouldn't understand, because she didn't care about what they said, but he did. He always had.

"Joey. What's up?" Carmine said.

"I was looking for you," Joey Dee said. "Thought we'd take a ride or something. You got the car?"

"Yeah," Carmine said. "I gotta make a stop up the Bronx for Benny. We could all take a ride." He looked at Josie Magro. He touched her arm. "What do you say, sweetheart? Wanna take a ride?"

"Sure," Josie Magro said.

"Don't you work today, Josie? Don't you work on Wednesdays?" Joey Dee said.

Josie Magro bent her arm and made a fist. She hit the upper part of her arm with her other hand. "What's it got to do with you?" she said. "Since when is what I do your business? Carmine asked me, not you."

"C'mon," Carmine said. "It's too nice a day to work. Right, Joey? It's a day to take a ride up the Bronx." He put an arm around Josie Magro. "Let's go," he said.

Joey Dee didn't want to go with Carmine and Josie Magro, not with the way Carmine was acting, but he didn't want to leave them alone either, just the two of them, all the way up to the Bronx. When Carmine and Josie Magro turned to go, he kicked the ironwork fence and tore the suede off the tips of his new shoes. "Bitch," Joey Dee said to himself. That's what Josie Magro was, a bitch, a bitch's daughter.

The three of them walked to Prince Street and turned down Sullivan, past Nicky Mole's cafe. Benny Scar was standing by the open door. He called to Joey Dee and told him to come inside.

The three of them stopped. "Go ahead," Joey Dee said. "I'll catch up."

"We'll wait," Carmine told him. He turned to Benny Scar. "Going up the Bronx now," he said. "Take care of that . . . you know."

"Why don't you go ahead?" Benny Scar said to Carmine. "Joey might be a while." He put his arm around Joey Dee. His face was close to Joey Dee's, the side of his face that had been torn open, the side with the scar.

"Yeah," Joey Dee said, waving a hand. "Go ahead, I got things to do anyway."

"Close the door," Benny Scar said when they got inside. Nicky Mole was at a table with some guy who sat with his hat in his hand, bending the brim, curling it between his fingers. Joey Dee was glad to see he wasn't wearing a tie.

Benny Scar told Joey Dee to wait. He didn't offer him coffee. Jumbo was behind the counter, not looking at Joey Dee, not looking at the table where Nicky Mole sat.

Only this morning Jumbo had told Benny Scar that even if another job didn't come through soon, he was leaving. He'd send his wife to work, he said. The book-binding factory was just around the corner from his house. It wouldn't kill her, but this job was killing him. He couldn't take it anymore, he told Benny Scar. This job made him feel like the floor was moving under him all the time, like it was going to open up and swallow him, all two hundred and fifty pounds of him.

"You mean, like you're going six feet under any day now, is that what you mean?" Benny Scar said.

"I'm just letting you know," Jumbo told him. "I appreciate the favor you done getting me in here, but I can't make it, Benny. I'm getting too nervous. I'm losing weight." Benny Scar didn't answer, but his face registered disgust.

When Nicky Mole finished with the guy with the hat, he looked up at Joey Dee as though he had been sitting there waiting just for him.

"Good to see you, kid," he said. "Sit down."

Joey Dee walked over to the table. Benny Scar pulled out a chair for Joey Dee and stood behind him when he sat down.

"You did like I told you? You brought the envelope?" Nicky Mole said.

"Yeah."

"She give you any trouble?"

"No, I gave it to her like you said and I left."

Nicky Mole touched Joey Dee's shoulder. "I like you, kid. You got qualities." He put both his hands on the table and spread his fingers. "I want you to do something else for me," Nicky Mole said. "I want you to pick her up sometimes and drive her where I tell you. You wait there, and you drive her back."

Joey Dee's throat closed. "I got no license, Nicky."

"You drive, no?"

"Yeah . . . but—"

"Don't you want to do this for me, Joey?"

"It ain't that," Joey Dee said. "I got no license."

"Don't worry about no license, as long as you can drive. You be here around ten tomorrow night. Benny will give you the car. You go to Sullivan Street and pick her up. Benny will tell you where to go after that." Nicky Mole turned away from Joey Dee and started talking to Fat Frankie in a dialect of the *bassi*. Joey Dee didn't understand it and didn't want to hear it in case they thought he did. When he got up, Benny Scar put an arm around his shoulders and walked him to the door.

"Ten o'clock," he said in Joey Dee's ear when he let him out.

SIX

Joey Dee was outside Nicky Mole's cafe at ten o'clock that night. The door was padlocked; the street was empty. Joey Dee shifted from one foot to the other and harbored the unlikely hope that nothing would come about. Benny Scar would not show up and he would catch the last movie at the Loew's Sheridan. He would go to the Louisiana Club on Third Street and have a drink with the bartender.

Benny Scar walked around the corner. Joey Dee stood up straight when he saw him coming. Benny Scar came alongside Joey Dee, and he signaled to him with his eyes. Benny Scar did not move his head, but shifted his eyes to where Joey Dee stood. His eyes told Joey Dee to follow. Benny Scar walked past Joey Dee and into the hallway of the building next to the cafe.

In the hallway, Benny Scar held up a set of keys. "There's a blue Buick parked on Varick Street," he told Joey Dee. "Drive it to Sullivan. Park in front of the church.

Take Route Nine south to Spring Lake. Follow the road to the end, to the ocean. Stop at the first house on the left."

Joey Dee closed his hand around the keys. Benny Scar didn't let go of the ring that held them. "Go straight there," Benny Scar said. "You don't talk to nobody, you don't stop nowhere, from the minute you walk out of here until you park that Buick back on Varick Street. You just keep going."

There was a blue Buick on Varick Street and the keys fit. Joey Dee drove it over to Sullivan and parked outside the church to wait for Carolina Magro to come down.

He had been waiting awhile when he had slid down in his seat and put his head back and closed his eyes. He didn't see her, but he heard the car door open and shut.

"So, it's you," she said from the backseat, "the courier, now the chauffeur."

Joey Dee started the engine. It sounded too loud in the quiet street. He thought he saw Vito Santero looking out of his window, but he couldn't be sure. He wondered if Angelina Lombardi was there, sitting in the dark with the lights out. He thought about Josie Magro upstairs in the apartment Carolina Magro had just left. It was the first of many nights he would park the blue Buick in front of the church to wait for Carolina Magro to slip into the backseat. He would always think the same thoughts.

Carolina would talk to him when she got in the car and Joey Dee would nod. She would get angry at him for this. "When I talk to you," she said, "I expect an answer."

"Yes," Joey Dee would say. "No," Joey Dee would say. "I don't know." He told himself that he would not talk to her. She would ask him question after question. Stupid questions, Joey Dee thought, just to make him answer, just to make him say something. Carolina Magro was used to making people do what she wanted them to do. She knew how to make them.

Joey Dee would pick her up and drive her to wherever Benny Scar told him. He would wait and drive her back. The destination always changed, and Joey Dee never knew where he was going until right before he left. He was nervous all the time. The worst was wondering about Josie and if she knew.

When Joey Dee would pick Carolina Magro up late at night, her mouth was so red he could see it even in the dark of the backseat. Joey Dee would drive her into New Jersey or Pennsylvania. He would drive her out to Long Island. He would see nothing but the back of her disappearing into a doorway.

After he had dropped her back on Sullivan Street, he would park the car and walk home, going in quietly so his father wouldn't hear, and sleeping into the day because he had been up so late and driven so far.

Joey Dee started going to church, not on Sunday and not for Mass, but in the early afternoon, when the church was empty except for the caretaker polishing the wooden pews. Inside the church Joey Dee would light candles. He would light them for Vito Santero, for Josie Magro, and for himself. He would light them for Sister Agnes, for Carolina Magro, and for Nicky Mole. He always lit the candles in threes. It was his way of doing things.

There was a statue Joey Dee liked to stand in front of and light the candles. It was a statue of God the Father with a long gray beard, sitting on a cloud filled with angels. God the Son sat at his right side. The statue was in the back of the church and it was the only one Joey Dee had ever seen of God the Father.

Joey Dee would stand in front of God the Father. He liked the idea of talking to the top man. "How did all this happen?" Joey Dee would ask him. "What am I going to do?"

"The commandments," Sister Agnes answered in his head. God the Father was too big a man to answer directly, Joey Dee figured.

The commandments, Joey Dee thought: Thou shalt not listen to retards on Sunday mornings. Thou shalt not take crazy girls to hotels on Thirty-third Street. Thou shalt not quit good jobs in frozen chicken factories.

Joey Dee would stand in the back of the church for a long time. If he were devout, Sister Agnes had told him once, he might see a statue move.

Nicky the Mole, meanwhile, was not himself, and his boys were surprised at the things he did. He made Fat Frankie take him to the jewelry exchange and the next day they noticed he was wearing a ring on the little finger of his left hand. It wasn't a diamond, which the boys thought it should have been, a man of his importance, but a sapphire, blue and milky, with a star that caught the light.

Nicky Mole ordered made-to-measure suits and shirts with long pointed collars. He went to Rocky's every day for a shave, and Rocky put his hands in the air when Nicky Mole left and talked more often about retiring to Florida.

Nicky Mole still sat in the cafe and took care of his business. He still played pinochle, but he sometimes forgot the cards he had played. The circles under his eyes darkened and he did not hit Fat Frankie on the side of his head with the same motivation. The boss was not himself and no one would talk about it. Fat Frankie did mention it to his wife, Dora, who refused to listen. It was enough for her to worry about what would happen to them if Nicky Mole ever went to jail. Dora didn't think about much else besides that and her four sons, to whom Nicky Mole sent cashmere coats every Christmas.

Josie Magro was in the hallway screaming up Joey Dee's name. His mother was in the kitchen making coffee. She stopped and pulled at his sheets and poked him with the wooden spoon.

"It's one o'clock," she said. "Get up. I told you to go in my bed when your father left for work. I can't get nothing done with you in here. I need the kitchen. And now that crazy Magro girl's calling for you. Get up and get rid of her, will you?"

Joey Dee got out of bed and poured himself coffee. He

drank it without milk or sugar. His eyes were half shut. He had gotten in past five A.M. When he opened the door and yelled down for Josie Magro to come up, his mother hit him with the spoon.

"What did you do that for?" she said. "Why'd you ask her up? What am I going to do with her? I'm trying to get you out of here, now I got to put up with her. The things you put me through, Joey. Someday . . ."

"C'mon, Ma," Joey Dee said. "Where's your hospitality?"

"Her mother's no good. She's probably no good either."

Joey Dee had left the door open. He looked up and saw Josie Magro in the doorway. She walked in without knocking. "Hello, Mrs. De Stefano," she said, showing all her teeth. They were magnificent teeth—like her mother's beauty, a gift from God.

Josie Magro sat down at the kitchen table. Joey Dee was in his shorts. Josie Magro was not embarrassed that he was in his shorts, that she had heard his mother call her mother no good, and her too. Joey Dee felt what he always felt when he saw Josie Magro, that she had no manners and no morals, but it didn't matter, because somehow he was stuck.

His mother would tell him that Josie Magro would ruin him, the way her mother had ruined Sonny Magro. "Dead in the street on a Sunday," she would tell him. "What a way to end up."

"Give Josie some coffee," he said. "She takes milk and sugar." He went into the living room to put on his pants. Through the opening between the rooms, he could see his mother take down a cup from a hook in the china closet and pour coffee for Josie Magro. Joey Dee took his time, but the silence was still there when he walked back in the kitchen.

"Listen Josie, you got to get out of here so I can get ready," Joey Dee told her. "I can't get washed or nothing with you in here. Wait for me downstairs."

"I'm drinking my coffee."

"Josie . . ."

"When I finish my coffee, I'll go down. What'd you ask me up for anyway?"

"I didn't want to leave you screaming in the hallway. That makes you mad, remember? When you call in the hallway and nobody answers you?"

Josie Magro stirred her coffee. She drank it slowly, deliberately, and when she was finished, she stood up. "Thanks for the coffee, Mrs. De Stefano." Those teeth again, Joey Dee thought. She brushed against him when she walked out.

Joey Dee's mother closed the door that Josie Magro had left open. "Where does she live? A barn?"

"C'mon, Ma."

Joey Dee's mother picked up Josie Magro's cup from the table and broke it on the fire escape out the kitchen window. She threw the pieces into the yard.

"What are you doing with her?" she said to Joey Dee. "So many nice girls in this neighborhood, you got to go with her?"

"Ma, you want her to hear you again?" Joey Dee moved the drainboard full of dishes off the bathtub and put it on the table.

"You can't take a bath now," his mother said. "What are you, crazy? I'm cooking. It's one o'clock. Get out of here."

"What am I gonna do? I gotta get washed."

"Go in your Aunt Julia's. Her boyfriend's gone by now. Go use her tub." She put the drainboard back.

Joey Dee went across the hall and let himself into Aunt Julia's. He had his own key. Aunt Julia sat and looked out the kitchen window while he took his bath.

Josie Magro was waiting on the stoop when Joey Dee came down. She was with Vito Santero, who had drool on his chin and was waving his arms in big circles. He stopped when he saw Joey Dee. He put his hands in the torn pockets of his coat.

"What's he saying?" Joey Dee said. "He telling you one of his crazy stories?" Joey Dee stepped off the stoop and grabbed Vito Santero's arm. "What are you doing all the way down here, Vito? Since when do you leave Sullivan Street?" Joey Dee looked at Vito Santero with his stone face.

Vito Santero opened his mouth but no sound came out. His cheeks were wet but Joey Dee couldn't tell if it was tears or snot, the way Vito kept rubbing his sleeve all over his face, under his nose and all over his face.

Vito backed away, down the street. He turned and started to run. Joey Dee started after him, but Josie Magro yelled for him to stop. Joey Dee stopped when she yelled at him. He didn't know what he was doing chasing Vito Santero down the street.

"What's with you?" Josie Magro said. "Why'd you scare him like that?" She was sitting with her knees apart and he could see up her skirt.

"I didn't mean nothing," Joey Dee said. "I'm nervous, that's all."

"With Vito?"

"No," he said. "It's got nothing to do with Vito. I'm just nervous. Why? You're so perfect?"

"Your mother's a doll," Josie Magro said. "How'd you get so lucky?"

Joey Dee leaned over, close to her. "Don't let's talk about mothers, Josie. You should shut your mouth when anybody talks about mothers."

Joey Dee thought she would hit him, ball her hand into a fist and hit him, hard. She could punch like a guy. Somebody had taught her. Sonny Magro? Joey Dee didn't know. There were things she never talked about.

But Josie Magro stood up and smoothed her skirt. She spit on the step in front of him and she walked off the stoop. He saw she was crying, and he wanted to rub her face with the sleeve of his shirt until her face looked like Vito's, all tears and snot and dirt, and then he wanted to take her someplace and make her forget what he had said, but he didn't move and she walked away. He watched her back. He watched for a long time because she walked slowly, as if nothing was bothering her, as if she were just walking down a street where nothing was happening.

When Joey Dee couldn't see her anymore, when she had turned the corner onto Sullivan Street and she was gone from his view, he kicked the stoop, and if he could have, if it was allowed, Joey Dee would have cried.

SEVEN

"**V**ito Santero is roaming," the ladies said. "Usually so quiet," they said, "always in front of Sammy One-eye's building, but lately, lately he's been roaming."

Joey Dee left Spring Street and walked up Sullivan toward Fourth Street Park. He was on the far side of Houston when Vito Santero saw him and ran toward him without looking. Trucks skidded and truck drivers leaned on their horns.

Joey Dee knew Vito was running to talk to him. Ever since he had told Joey Dee his secret, Vito had become attached to him, bound to him in a way that Joey Dee didn't understand but felt as strongly as he felt anything.

Vito Santero was breathing hard when he reached Joey Dee. The truck drivers were cursing his mother, but Vito paid no attention. He put his arms around Joey Dee. He put his face next to Joey Dee's face. Joey Dee stepped back and held Vito Santero's arms.

"What's with you, Vito? Why'd you run away before?"

"That was her," Vito whispered. "You know who that was?"

"Who? Josie? You talking about Josie?"

Vito squeezed his eyes shut. "That's his daughter. Sonny Magro, up the roof, you know, Sonny Magro . . ."

Joey Dee shook Vito Santero before he let go of him. "Vito, if you don't stop . . ."

"See, see, I knew you'd get mad. You always get mad. That's why I ran away. You always get mad anything to do with Sonny Magro, but Joey, I seen more things. I seen Sonny Magro's wife go out at night. I seen a car come get her."

"Vito, I keep telling you to mind your own business. Why can't you do that, Vito? Why can't you forget all about Sonny Magro and the roof and just sweep the sidewalk and move the ashcans for Sammy One-eye like you're supposed to?"

"She's so pretty, Sonny Magro's wife."

"Yeah, I know, Vito, but that don't mean you should watch for her out the window. Why are you doing that, Vito?"

"I can't sleep no more, Joey. I see things when I sleep so I get up and I look out the window. I'm telling you, Joey, because I tell you everything. You're my friend. You and Sister Agnes."

"Yeah, the Holy Trinity."

"What, Joey? What'd you say?"

"Nothing, Vito, forget it."

"Where's Sister Agnes, Joey? You told me, but I forget. Where is she?"

"Why can't you forget everything else the way you forget that?" Joey Dee said. He put a hand in his shirt pocket and took out a cigarette. "She's upstate, Vito, where they keep the old nuns, in the country."

"She's not old . . ."

"No, but she's special. They keep special nuns up there, too, with the old ones."

"Does she like it up there, Joey? Is there kids up there? She won't like it up there with no kids."

"There's everything up there, Vito. Sister Agnes likes it a lot. You ask Father Giannini."

"Where you going now, Joey, huh? Where?"

"Noplace."

"You wanna stay with me? I got a chair. Sammy One-eye gave me a chair. I put it in the alley between the buildings. You wanna sit in my chair, Joey?"

"Maybe later, Vito. I'll come by later."

"I sit in my chair and I talk to everybody that passes. I like that."

"But you don't say nothing, right, Vito? You don't say secrets?"

"About Sonny Magro and Nicky Mole on the roof? No, Joey." Vito Santero shook his head.

Sister Agnes had a bank, Joey Dee remembered. A little black boy with a begging bowl sat on top of it, and his head bobbed when you put in a penny for the missions. Sister Agnes collected pennies for the missions every day before lunch. She got the children's pennies before they could go outside and spend them in Lemons' candy store. They would put their pennies in to see the little black boy bob his head and because Sister Agnes made them.

"C'mon, Vito," Joey Dee said. "I'll cross you and you can go sit in your chair." Vito Santero was still shaking his head, smiling at the feeling of his head moving around on his neck, while Joey Dee pulled him across Houston Street and down Sullivan. He left him sitting in his chair, bobbing his head like the little black boy on Sister Agnes's bank.

Joey Dee didn't know what to think of first, what to take care of. He couldn't forget Josie Magro crying. He couldn't believe how seeing her cry had made him feel. He didn't figure on this, his feelings for Josie Magro getting more and more complicated.

In the beginning he thought he was just getting some, more than the other guys. Joey Dee had always gotten more. He had Sister Agnes touching him when all of them were still touching themselves. "You must be blessed," Carmine had said when he found out about Sister Agnes. "A nun, for Chrissakes, and she ain't bad-looking."

Joey Dee had not told about Sister Agnes. He was not a guy who talked, even then, but Mikey Bats and Carmine had seen the red in his face and they had seen Sister Agnes's hands on him, smoothing the skirt of his cassock, pushing the tails of his shirt into the front of his pants.

Joey Dee thought about telling Josie Magro what he felt, what he thought, but he would have to tell her everything, about Sonny Magro, about Carolina. He thought about going to Nicky Mole and telling him he wouldn't drive Carolina Magro anymore. He saw himself in the cafe, standing up, Nicky Mole sitting down, his spoon circling the little cup filled with black coffee.

Nicky Mole wouldn't speak. He would stir his coffee and wait for Joey Dee to say something. He would already be angry that Joey Dee had come without being called, had come to see him for a reason he couldn't know. Nicky Mole knew everything. The neighborhood believed this. It was his power and his strength.

Benny Scar would be standing very close to Joey Dee while he stood in front of Nicky Mole. "What is it, kid?" Nicky Mole would say.

"I can't pick up Carolina Magro anymore," Joey Dee would say.

"What's the problem?" Nicky Mole would say, like he was interested in Joey Dee's problems, like he worried about Joey Dee and would take care of whatever was on his mind.

And then what would Joey Dee say? That he knew about Sonny Magro on the roof, that Vito Santero had told him? That he loved Josie Magro? That Carolina Magro sat in the back of the Buick with her skirt hiked up and touched the back of his neck while he was driving?

Joey Dee stopped the scene in his head. He was almost to Fourth Street when he turned around and walked back down Sullivan. Vito Santero was sitting out in front of Sammy One-eye's building, but Joey Dee was up the stoop and in the hallway before Vito Santero could get off his chair. Before Vito Santero could move, Joey Dee was up the four flights of stairs to Josie Magro's apartment.

Carolina Magro opened the door. It was two in the afternoon and she wasn't dressed. She stood in the doorway and stared at him.

"I'm looking for Josie," Joey Dee said.

Carolina opened the door and stood aside. "Come in, then." She shut the door behind him. They were alone in the kitchen. Joey Dee looked through into the living room. There was no one there."

"I'm looking for Josie," he said.

"You said that."

"Where is she?" Joey Dee felt the sweat start under his collar.

"She went out."

"I'll come back," he said.

"Why don't you wait?" Carolina Magro said. "She should be here soon."

Joey Dee hesitated. The kitchen felt small. He felt as though Carolina Magro was standing against him, as though her body was touching his. "I'll come back later," he said.

Carolina Magro's mouth was very red. "Sit down," she told him. "You're nervous for such a young kid. What's wrong with you?"

Joey Dee sat down in a kitchen chair. He tried to look relaxed. He put one elbow on the table. He took a cigarette from the pack she held out to him.

"I hate this apartment," she said. "I'm in here all day. It's like a goddamn dungeon. I only get out . . . well, you know when I get out." Carolina put a cigarette in her mouth and leaned over for Joey Dee to light it. He struck a match and she cupped her hand around his and guided the tip of the cigarette into the flame.

"Why don't you go out?" he said. She pulled on the cigarette. He saw the red stain her lipstick left on the filter.

"Where?" she said. "For what? So those hags on the park

bench can throw their cheap curses? I can't be bothered. When I get out of here, it's going to be for good."

Joey Dee smoked his cigarette and worried about the ash on the end of it. He was puffing so hard that the ash was ready to fall.

"What do you want with Josie?" Carolina Magro said. "You take her out?"

The ash fell off Joey Dee's cigarette. It fell on his pants and onto the floor. "We see each other," he said.

"Tough guy," Carolina Magro said. "You're such a tough guy. What do you have to do with Nicky? Where'd he get you?"

Joey Dee wanted to tell her that he didn't know and he wished it would stop. He loved her daughter, but he loved her, too, in some awful way. And did she know that Nicky Mole had killed her husband? Another ash fell on his pants. Joey Dee stood up. "I have to go," he said to her. "I'll come by later."

Carolina came around the table. The door was locked from the inside and she stood against it. She put her arms around him, her hands on his back, under his shirt. She put her very red mouth against the side of his neck.

Someone pulled at the door, then knocked. Carolina Magro moved away. It seemed to Joey Dee she took forever. She pushed the tails of Joey Dee's shirt into the front of his pants. She rubbed her hand against the red her mouth had left on his skin.

Carolina Magro unlocked the door from the inside and Josie Magro opened it. She looked at Joey Dee. "He came to see you," Carolina Magro said. "He was just leaving, but now he can stay."

"What are you doing here?" Josie Magro said. "I don't believe it. What do you want?"

Joey Dee felt like throwing up, the way he felt that Sunday when Vito Santero told him the story about Sonny Magro up the roof. "I want to talk to you. I figured you'd be home," he said. "Can we go downstairs?"

"You're here now," Josie Magro said.

"She's right," Carolina Magro said. "You're here now. Sit down. I'll make some coffee."

Joey Dee went down into the street alone. Vito Santero was still in his chair on the sidewalk.

"Joey," he said. "Where'd you go? Where you been?"

"To a tea party, Vito."

"That's nice," Vito said. "You always have a nice time, right, Joey?"

Joey Dee took out one of his white linen handkerchiefs, spread it out on the stoop and sat down.

"What are you doing that for?" Vito Santero said. "You're gonna get your handkerchief all dirty. I sweep and I sweep, but the steps are still dirty. What you gonna get your handkerchief all dirty for?"

Joey Dee put his elbows on his knees. He held his head in his hands. "You know, Vito," he said, "maybe Sister Agnes did you a favor."

When Joey Dee passed Nicky Mole's cafe on the way home, Benny Scar gave him the high sign. "Tonight," Benny Scar said.

Joey Dee never knew ahead of time when he would have to pick up Carolina Magro. It was expected that he would make himself available, and in some unthinking way, Joey Dee did that. He passed by the cafe all the time. He did this anyway, the cafe being between his house and everywhere else he ever went, but he was conscious of the cafe now, and of how often he passed it.

He would pass by the cafe and Benny Scar would tell him when, and he would pass by the cafe again and Benny Scar would tell him where. Joey Dee had a fake license that Fat Frankie had made up for him, and he had a bad sense of direction.

That night when he picked her up, Joey Dee felt worse than he usually did. Carolina Magro got in the car, and when they had passed Houston Street, out of the boundaries of the neighborhood, Carolina Magro touched the back of his neck with her gloved hand. She outlined his ear with her fingers. Joey Dee felt the rope around his neck, Nicky Mole's big fingers squeezing his throat.

"You're always so quiet," Carolina Magro said. Joey Dee was angry with her, for making him nervous, for teasing him, for being Josie Magro's mother. "You know," she said, "you're too sensitive. It won't get you anywhere, believe me. You should grow up. You'll never make it."

"What are you talking about?" he said.

"Listen, you think all this is easy for me, that I have no feelings? I've got a daughter to raise alone. I've got the *stregas* on the park bench waiting to take out my eyes. They've been waiting for me all my life." She had leaned forward to tell him this, but now she sat back. Joey Dee could see her skirt high on her legs. He could see her in the rearview mirror. "This neighborhood," she said. "There's only one way to do things, from the beginning to the end, when Gambino lays you out in a box you can't afford. Well, let me tell you, I'm not like the rest of them. I don't belong here. I never belonged here."

Joey Dee thought she was crying. She had her face down and he couldn't see. He thought about pulling the car over on the West Side Highway and about holding her and how she would put her hands under his clothes, but when she lifted her face he could see she wasn't crying but only fooling with her makeup. She seemed to have forgotten he was there. He was her chauffeur.

Joey Dee pulled up to the address Benny Scar had given him and he got out to open the door for Carolina Magro. She swung both her legs out the door and put her hand up for him to help her out. She said something into his ear that he couldn't understand. He knew Nicky Mole was inside waiting for her. He wondered if she had been Nicky Mole's girl long before Sonny Magro was found dead in the street on a Sunday. Joey Dee watched her go inside.

He fell asleep in the car. When she came out, it was almost four-thirty. He woke up when she slammed the car door. "Let's go," she said. There were circles under her eyes.

"Does Josie know?" he said to her.

Carolina leaned forward in the seat and she touched his hair. "Does Josie know what?" she said.

Joey Dee kept his eyes straight ahead. "Nothing," he said. He looked into the blackness and imagined the desert.

On Sunday Joey Dee saw Mikey Bats on the corner where they always stood after the Mass let out. Mikey Bats waved and Joey Dee went over to him. "Where's Carmine?" he said.

"I dunno. I thought he'd be here. It's so goddamn hot, ain't it, Joey? We should go someplace."

They saw Carmine then, coming up the street, from the direction of Nicky Mole's cafe. Mikey Bats called to him and Carmine came over and hit him on the shoulder. They shook hands and Carmine grabbed Mikey Bats in a bear hug.

"Hey," Joey Dee said. "You weren't in church."

"I had some things to do. You know how it is."

"Even on Sunday they got you running?" Mikey Bats said. "You don't even get no rest on Sunday?"

"It ain't so bad. I got money in my pocket. I can't say that for you two."

"I'm doing OK," Joey Dee said. "Money ain't everything."

"It ain't nothing, either," Carmine said. "It's up to you. I can get you started in action anytime you want. Benny Scar asks about you all the time, Joey. There's always a place for you."

"Thanks, Carmine, but I told you, I ain't interested. Maybe I'm gonna get out of here."

"Out? Where? You going someplace, Joey?" Mikey Bats said. He pulled on his tie to loosen it and opened his collar.

"Yeah, maybe I'm going someplace."

"Someplace far? Like California? A lot of guys are out in California."

"What can you do out there?" Carmine said. "You think it's easy getting started?"

"I was thinking of the desert," Joey Dee said. "I was thinking of Vegas. I could probably get something out there, something clean, anyway."

Carmine stretched his shoulders back. "I like it right here," he said. "I ain't never had it so good."

Joey Dee looked away, over at the ladies on the park bench. They were sitting with their knees apart, making a breeze with their handkerchiefs. It was too hot to go home. They would wait and they would watch. It was early and it was too hot a day to go straight up the house.

"So what do you say we do something?" Joey Dee said.

"Yeah," Mikey Bats agreed. "It's so goddamn hot."

"Let's go to the beach," Carmine said. "I got the car. We'll eat out there in Brooklyn."

"OK. We'll meet here in an hour," Joey Dee said.

Joey Dee went home and got his bathing suit and a towel. His mother pulled his hair. "Your Aunt Carmella's coming," she said. "Your cousins are coming. You're supposed to be here. They want to see you."

"Ma, they don't want to see me. You want them to see me." He put a piece of cake in his mouth. The powdered sugar fell on his shirt, on the floor. He kissed her and left powdered sugar on her face. He went out the door, and all the way down the stairs he could hear her calling after him. He walked up Sullivan Street slapping his towel against the signs and fire escape ladders hanging off the buildings, leaping high to reach them.

He passed Vito Santero sitting on his chair in front of Sammy One-eye's building. There was a pillow on the chair. There were tassels on the edges of the pillow. Vito Santero saw Joey Dee and got off the chair. "Where you going, Joey?"

"I'm in a hurry, Vito." Joey Dee thought for one second about taking Vito Santero to the beach. Vito would start to drool if Joey Dee said for him to come. His nose would run and he would wipe it with his sleeve.

I'm getting soft in the head, Joey Dee thought, and he forgot about it. He could see Mikey Bats standing near the chain link fence of the park. Carmine wasn't there yet, and Joey Dee slowed down. He wanted to arrive last. The most important guy was the one you waited for.

He was almost there when he saw Carmine coming across Houston Street with Josie Magro. Mikey Bats had spotted Joey Dee and was waving. He yelled for Joey Dee to hurry up, that it was late already.

Joey Dee couldn't figure what was going on with Carmine. He thought about choking Josie Magro. "What's she doing here?" he said to Carmine when they all met at the corner.

"C'mon, Joey, what's the big deal? We're going to the beach. There's some law says she can't come?" Josie Magro looked at Joey Dee and formed her mouth around a vulgar word.

"Nobody said nothing about girls, Carmine. Where do you come off bringing a girl?" Joey Dee waited. He watched Carmine's face. He wanted to hear him say Josie Magro wasn't his girl, that he had just met her on the street and asked her to come. He wanted to hear that it was all a coincidence and that he shouldn't think about it, but Carmine just looked up and said he was sorry. "I didn't figure . . ." he told Joey Dee.

"Yeah, you never figure. You're some kind of tough guy now, you got a few bucks in your pocket?"

"Why don't you shut up?" Josie Magro said. "Who the hell are you anyway? What do you care if I come or not?"

"Don't take it personal, Josie. I don't give a damn that it's you. It's the principle. Nobody said nothing about girls."

"It's hot," Mikey Bats said. "We're supposed to go to the beach. Let's go. It's late already."

"You banging her too?" Joey Dee said.

Josie Magro came at him and Joey Dee put up his arms. "You bastard," she said. Carmine held her back.

"For Chrissakes, Joey," Carmine said. "What's with you? Why'd you say something like that?" He stood behind Josie Magro. He had his arms around her shoulders.

"You should drop dead," Josie Magro said to Joey Dee. "You should just fucking die."

"C'mon, Joey," Mikey Bats said.

"I ain't going anymore," Joey Dee said.

"Good," Josie Magro told him. "Who needs you? It's Carmine's car."

Joey Dee turned and left. "Joey," Carmine said. "C'mon, don't be like that." Joey Dee kept walking. He dragged the towel along the fences and blackened store windows. It was torn and dirty when he got home and his mother started on him, but then she forgot about the towel. She was glad because he was home and her sister and his cousins were coming and he would be there, and she could show him off, her son.

EIGHT

Joey Dee went to bed Sunday night after his cousins left and he stayed there. He needed time to think. His mother fed him soup with pastina and made plasters to put on his chest. He told her his head didn't hurt and that the alcohol rag made him dizzy, but she tied it around his forehead anyway.

He knew Benny Scar was looking for him, standing outside Nicky Mole's cafe, watching for him through the crack in the door, peeking over the black paint on the windows. Benny Scar was waiting for Joey Dee to come by to give him the high sign.

Joey Dee couldn't believe that Josie Magro was with Carmine. He couldn't figure it. No one would touch Josie Magro with a ten-foot pole the whole time they were growing up. She was crazy, the ladies said, *"un po'pazza."* How Joey Dee had started seeing her had been an acci-

dent of fate. His mother would have sighed and crossed herself to hear him say this.

He had been cutting school. He had done that a lot before
he dropped out, and he had been walking on the West Side,
all the way over, near the river, where they parked the trucks
at night. He saw Josie Magro sitting way out on the pier near
Christopher Street. He couldn't tell from where he was that it
was Josie Magro. He just saw a girl out at the end of Pier 42,
sitting with her arms around her legs, not moving at all. He
stood there and watched her for a long time. He was still
there when she got up, and when she passed him, he realized
who she was.

Josie Magro stopped and said hello. She stood there, her
arms crossed in front of her. It was summer and her arms
were bare and tanned up to the beginning of her shirtsleeve.
A truck-driver tan, the kind of tan you got working with your
arm out a window.

Joey Dee liked that. The neighborhood girls would go to
Coney Island and spend the whole day sitting with the straps
of their bathing suits down so their tans would be even. They
couldn't move because their bathing suits would fall down
and they couldn't put up their straps because of the tan lines,
but Josie Magro's arms were white above her shirtsleeves.

Joey Dee was interested. "You know me?" he said.

"Yeah, I know you . . . Joey. They call you Joey Dee."

He liked that she knew who he was. "Where are you
going?" he asked her.

"Home. I was just sitting by the water."

He didn't tell her that he knew that, that he had been
watching her for a long time. "I'll walk with you," Joey Dee
said. It was a question but he didn't say it that way. She
shrugged.

They had walked for hours that first day, until he could go
home and his mother would think he had been at school. She
told him her mother didn't keep track of things like that.
They had hardly talked. He had bought her lunch in a place
on Tenth Avenue in the thirties, far from where anyone who

knew them would be. He had done that to her even then, that first day.

Joey Dee was so cool back then. He had his crew, Mikey Bats, Carmine. They had followed him around back then, did everything he said. Now he was losing everything and going nowhere fast.

His mother came in with something foul-smelling to rub on his chest and he pretended he was asleep. She opened his eyes with her fingers. "Somebody's looking for you," she said. "Somebody's calling for you in the hallway."

"Who? Josie Magro?"

"Not her, thank God," his mother said. "It's a boy's voice."

"Don't answer," Joey Dee said. "I don't want to see nobody. I don't feel good."

He got up and looked out the window to see who it was. He saw Carmine come out of the hallway. He thought he had probably come to apologize about Sunday, to tell Joey Dee that it had been a mistake, that Josie Magro wasn't nothing. Thinking this made Joey Dee feel important, like they were still a crew and he was still the boss. But he watched the way Carmine walked along Spring Street, his head up, hat cocked to the side, and he realized that Carmine had come to find him for Benny Scar, for Fat Frankie, for Nicky Mole.

He felt dizzy then. He really felt sick. When his mother touched his forehead with her lips, she frowned and said she was calling Rosina Scarpacci, who had taken over when Donna Vecchio died. "*Mala fattura*," Joey Dee's mother said. She wasn't taking any chances.

"Forget it, Ma," Joey Dee said. "I'm fine."

"Let her come, Joey, please. I don't like this. You're sick but you're not sick. It's the *malocchio*, I know it. What can it hurt to call Rosina? Let her come, for me."

"Ma, please, the last time she came, she stuck her two fingers in my eyes. I thought I was blind."

"You got better, didn't you?"

"Ma, I wasn't sick."

"Why did I call her then, you weren't sick?"

"I don't remember. You had a dream or something."

"So let me call her. This time you're sick. Just to make me feel good."

"No, Ma, please."

"Joey . . ."

"Ma, the old man hates this stuff. He hates Rosina Scarpacci. 'That witch,' he calls her. You got enemies in this building, Ma. You know who I mean." He moved his head in the direction of Aunt Julia's apartment. "She'd love to get something on you. You know she can't, you're too good, but she'd love to tell the old man you had Rosina Scarpacci up here."

Joey Dee's mother put a hand on his forehead. "You really don't feel too bad?" she asked him.

"Ma, I'm fine. I'm tired, that's all. I stay out too late, but I'm fine."

"OK," she said. She kissed his hairline. She kissed his eyes. "Rest, I'll make you something nice."

When Joey Dee finally left the house, he went to Rocky's for a haircut. He thought about getting a shave, something to help him face the world. Sammy One-eye was in the barber chair when he got there. Joey Dee sat down to wait and flipped through a magazine of naked girls with very red mouths.

Sammy One-eye was talking to Rocky about Vito Santero. He was telling Rocky that something was wrong. "There's always been something wrong with Vito Santero," Rocky said. "He was born that way."

"No, I don't mean that," Sammy One-eye said. "I know he's *stunade* in the head, but he was always quiet. He'd hang around quiet-like. I'd have to tell him all the time to move the ashcans. He was kind of lazy. But he's changed. He's nervous like a cat, always moving those ashcans, rolling them back and forth from the sidewalk to the alley. I been getting complaints about the noise. That's why I got him that chair, so he can sit still.

"And if he's not rolling those ashcans, he's up walking around the roof. 'I gotta take care of the birds, Sammy,' he tells me when I ask him what he's doing. I tell him, 'Vito, I know about birds. You don't have to be up there all the time.' He walks around up there. Angelina Lombardi's on the top floor and she hears him. She's always complaining. 'I'm on the top floor because I don't want nobody walking on my head,' she tells me. 'You think I should be up here? All these stairs? That's why I never get out.'

"Then she tells me he talks to himself up there. I told him, 'Vito, why you gotta walk around? Why you gotta talk loud? You wanna be with the birds, fine, stay still, be quiet.' I'd give him a chair up there, too, but it makes holes in the roof and then I get leaks. He tells me he talks to the birds and he's gotta walk around when he talks. I don't know why I bother telling him things. Who knows what he can understand? It's no picnic, that building. It ain't one thing, it's another."

When Joey Dee's turn came up, he got a haircut and skipped the shave. The girl came over and said Carmine Menotti had an appointment for a manicure, but she had time to give him one first if he wanted. She put her hand on his arm. Joey Dee said no, but thanks anyway. He paid Rocky and left. He didn't especially want to see Carmine.

Vito Santero wasn't in front of Sammy One-eye's building when he got there. The chair was near the entrance to the alley. Joey Dee went inside the building and took the stairs up to the roof. The tar on the roof was wet from the heat and stuck to Joey Dee's shoes.

Joey Dee heard Vito Santero before he saw him. The birds were out, perched on the roof of the pigeon house, lined along the parapet wall. Vito Santero was walking back and forth on Angelina Lombardi's head, talking out loud. He was saying how Sonny Magro had come home late and how Fat Frankie and Benny Scar and Nicky Mole had taken him up the roof.

Vito Santero said that he was there, too, up the roof. He had put himself inside the pigeon house when he heard them coming. Nobody knew what had happened that night, he said, nobody except him and Joey Dee and Father Giannini. He had told them because they knew where Sister Agnes was, and Vito Santero loved Sister Agnes.

Vito Santero waved his arms and told his story to the birds. He shouted it into the wind, and when he was finished, he went back to the beginning. Joey Dee leaned up against the roof door. The pigeons made pigeon sounds and shifted on their feet.

Joey Dee's shoes were stuck in the melting tar of the roof. He could hear Vito Santero crying great big loud sobs. He knew Vito's eye, the bad one, was moving around crazy in his head.

"I don't want to," Vito Santero was saying between sobs, "but I'm going to. I'm going to use the handkerchief Joey Dee gave me. Look at this," he said. He held out the white linen handkerchief to the birds on the parapet wall. He held it up to the birds in the sky. "My friend Joey Dee gave it to me. He knows the story. I told him . . . and Father Giannini. I told Father Giannini, too."

Joey Dee thought he would throw up. He looked out over the parapet wall to the roof of the church, to the bell tower. There were birds sitting on the roof of the bell tower. Pigeons, Joey Dee thought. We're all pigeons.

Vito Santero was still talking. "Joey Dee and me," he was saying to the birds on the radio antenna above his head, "we had Sister Agnes in school. Sister Agnes liked Joey Dee. She sent him on errands through the tunnel under the street. Sister Agnes liked children. She gave us crayons and we would color pictures of children. We would color their little faces brown and black and yellow and red. Sister Agnes taught us songs." Vito Santero put his arms up to heaven and started to sing.

Joey Dee left Vito Santero on the roof singing. He looked down at his shoes. They were spectators, brown and white, and there was tar in the perforations that made a pattern on the tips. All the little holes were filled with tar.

Joey Dee stopped to look at them more closely. He didn't realize he was in front of Carolina Magro's door. She opened it and caught him standing there, looking at his shoes. Joey Dee was embarrassed.

"I can get that off," she said.

He didn't think but turned and went inside with her. He took off the shoes and gave them to her. She went into the other room and left him sitting at the kitchen table. He smelled kerosene.

Joey Dee sat there without moving, the way he sat in the shoemaker's little booth with the swinging door because the shoemaker had his shoes and he couldn't go anywhere without them.

When Carolina Magro brought the shoes back they were cleaner, but the holes were still filled with tar. His mother would get the tar out of the holes, Joey Dee thought. He suddenly wanted to get out, to be home with his mother.

"You still seeing Josie?" Carolina Magro asked.

"Why?" Joey Dee said. He smoothed his sock with both hands, the way a woman would, before he put his foot into his shoe.

"Because she's seeing some guy, Carmine. Takes her all over. Buys her some nice things."

"I bet he does," Joey Dee said. He couldn't get his other shoe on. The laces were tight and his fingers were clumsy. Carolina Magro laughed at him. Joey Dee's face was hot.

"You're a real tough guy," she said. She kneeled down and took the shoe in her hand. She opened the laces and slipped it on his foot. She rested his foot on the top of her leg and tied his shoe.

"What were you doing up the roof?" she said to him when she stood up.

"I got birds up there," Joey Dee said.

Carolina Magro moved nearer. "Sammy One-eye doesn't like anyone going up the roof. I hear him all the time complaining to the Santero woman about her kid going up there. What's his name? The crazy one who moves the ashcans?"

"Vito. His name's Vito, and he's not crazy, he's slow."

"Yeah, I know," Carolina Magro said. "He was born that way."

"No, he wasn't. He was OK until . . ."

But Carolina Magro didn't hear him. She opened the door and waited by it. "You'd better get out of here," she said.

Joey Dee got up from the table and walked over to the door. He passed very close to her. She held the door and shut it behind him. He could hear her locking it from the inside.

NINE

Joey Dee heard Vito Santero on the stairs below him, and he stopped and waited on the landing outside Carolina Magro's door. When he heard the hallway door slam shut, he ran down the stairs, jumping four steps at each landing, and went out into the street.

Vito Santero was rolling an ashcan back and forth along the sidewalk. He didn't see Joey Dee until he grabbed the collar of his coat.

Vito's bad eye was moving crazy in his head. He started blinking and his mouth hung open. Joey Dee didn't like the way Vito Santero looked. He didn't look good at all.

"What are you doing, Vito?" he said to him. "Are you doing like I told you?"

Vito Santero put his hand up to touch Joey Dee's, to get it off the collar of his coat. "I ain't done nothing, Joey, nothing."

"Why do you go up the roof all the time? What do you do up there?"

"I take care of the birds, Joey. You never go up there any-more. I wait for you to come, to fly the birds, but you never come."

Joey Dee couldn't answer. He let go of Vito's coat collar. He hadn't been up the roof since Vito told him about Sonny Magro. He was afraid he would see the blood. He still saw it in the street sometimes, on the curb in front of the church.

"I take care of the birds," Vito Santero said again.

"You talk to them, Vito. Only crazy people talk to birds."

Vito Santero started waving his arms. "I ain't crazy," he said. "I ain't. I'm slow, that's all. My mother keeps telling me, 'Stay off the roof.' Sammy One-eye, he don't want me on the roof. Angelina Lombardi don't want me up the roof. But I go up there anyway. I gotta take care of the birds."

Mikey Bats and Carmine came up Sullivan Street and stopped where Joey Dee and Vito Santero were standing. "Why don't you leave this guy alone?" Carmine kidded Joey Dee, putting an arm around Vito's shoulder.

"How's everything, Carmine?" Joey Dee said.

"Can't complain. I've been looking for you. Me and Mikey was just saying we don't see you no more."

"Bullshit, Carmine. You saw me Sunday, remember?"

"Benny Scar's looking for you," Mikey Bats said. "Fat Frankie's looking for you, too. Everbody's looking for you, Joey."

Carmine shook his head. "He's right, Joey. I was in the cafe and your name came up."

"About what?"

"I don't know, Joey. I don't ask questions. I keep telling you that, but you don't want to hear."

"Listen, I gotta go," Joey Dee said. He started to move away.

Josie Magro turned the corner. She stopped to look at them. "Excuse me," she said and pushed past.

Joey Dee grabbed her arm. He didn't care about any of them, what they would think. The ladies were sitting on the park bench, their fat knees bulging over their garters, but he didn't look over to see if they were watching.

"I have to talk to you," Joey Dee said.

Josie pulled away and went up the stoop. Joey Dee followed her. He caught the second door into the hallway before she could close it. "Please, Josie, I want to tell you something."

"Come up, then."

"Your mother's home."

"So what?" She looked at him and narrowed her eyes.

"I have to talk to you alone."

"The roof," she said. "Let's go up the roof."

"No."

"What's with you?" she said.

"What's with you and Carmine? What's going on?"

"Joey, do me a favor and drop dead. That's what you want to talk about? Me and Carmine? What's wrong with Carmine? You don't see him walking away from me every time some old lady looks over from the park bench."

"You're no good, Josie. You know that?"

"I thought you wanted to tell me something, Joey."

"That's it. That's what I wanted to tell you."

"Good, then you're finished."

The door took a long time to close behind her. Through the glass, Joey Dee watched her disappear inside the building. He waited there, listening to the sound of her climbing one flight of stairs after the other. When she reached her floor and stopped, he held his breath in the sudden silence, and then he turned and left, pushing past Mikey Bats and Carmine and Vito Santero standing outside. He could feel his face getting hot, the ladies watching him from the park bench.

Joey Dee went up the street, up the steps of the church, and in the side door. It was cool and dark. His statue was there, God the Father, and he lit three candles in front of it.

Joey Dee sat in a side pew. He saw the red light over the confessional box and Father Giannini's name over the door.

Joey Dee had thought that if Vito Santero kept quiet no one would know about Sonny Magro. No one was trying to find out what had happened, who had done this terrible thing to Sonny Magro. Joey Dee had expected it would all be forgotten in time, but now Vito had told Father Giannini. Joey Dee didn't know what that meant, but he didn't like it.

Father Giannini's sermon that Sunday had been about the woman who spread stories and asked the priest for forgiveness. The priest had told her to split a feather pillow and open it to the wind and then gather up the feathers and bring them to him. When she came back and said she couldn't, he told her that it was the same with stories. They could never be taken back once they were told. The sermon had made Joey Dee shift on his feet in the back of the church.

Joey Dee kneeled down and put his head in his hands. He thought about Josie Magro. He should forget her. He thought about the last time they had been together in the hotel on Thirty-third Street near Macy's with the afternoon light coming in through the sides of the window shade. He wondered if she was going there with Carmine. He tried to remember if it was Carmine who had told him about that hotel.

Father Giannini came out of the confessional box and took his name from the slot over the door. He passed by the pew where Joey Dee sat and stopped. "Do you want to confess?" he said.

Joey Dee looked up. "No, Father. I'm just sitting." Father Giannini put a hand on Joey Dee's shoulder. The movie priest, they called him. He had been in a movie once, playing a priest who baptized a baby on the side altar.

Joey Dee was laying low again, but he couldn't take to his bed. The act was getting tired. He started going up the roof. He spent time with the birds. He and Vito Santero had built a pigeon house on Sammy One-eye's roof against the parapet wall. It was big enough for a man to stand in. There were rooms inside with boxes that fit two birds each. Joey Dee had put in ventilation and tapped into Angelina Lombardi's electricity. There were windows with screens that they covered with wooden shutters in the winter. Vito Santero kept it clean and carried up big bags of feed from the bird store on Avenue A.

Joey Dee was comfortable on the roof again. There was no blood that he could see. He flew the birds like he used to. He would chase them up with the stick. He would make circles in the sky above his head with the stick, the handkerchief tied to the end of it turning in the wind. The birds would spiral higher and higher into the air. They would catch other birds in the vortex of the circle.

Joey Dee's birds would catch homers and tiplits and flights, whitecaps and plainheads, redbeards and black tigers. He would count them and take the best birds with the colors he liked and put them two by two in the boxes at night. It was a hot September and the pigeon eggs would hatch in only eighteen days. Some of them were especially beautiful.

He gave three to Vito Santero, who named them, but Vito wouldn't tell Joey Dee the names. He said it was a secret. Joey Dee never named his birds. He knew all of them, could tell which ones in a flock were his, but they were still just birds. Vito Santero kept his three birds in a separate part of the coop. He kept them inside when the hawks gathered on the high buildings surrounding the tenements. He fed them pieces of fruit.

From Sammy One-eye's roof, where Joey Dee kept the birds, he could see the roof of the church. The birds would sit there on the peaked roof of the church for a long time. Joey Dee would throw feed to bring them down. At night, he would put them in their boxes and they would put their heads under their wings, hidden from the world. Joey Dee would stay up there long after it was dark.

At first Joey Dee had kept the birds on the roof of his building on Spring Street, but the ladies complained that the birds shit on the clean sheets they hung out to dry on the roof. "If you had a job," Joey Dee's father had said, "you wouldn't have time for birds. Get rid of the birds," he had said, so Joey Dee had moved them to Sammy One-eye's roof. Vito Santero had followed him up and down the stairs the day he moved the birds. He had helped Joey Dee build the pigeon coop and he had come back every day after that to take care of the birds.

Sammy One-eye wouldn't let the ladies hang clothes on his roof. He didn't want them up there, walking on the roof with their shoes that made punctures in the tar, going up there to hang clothes and then staying to talk and take the sun. Sammy One-eye didn't want anybody on his roof, but he let Joey Dee keep the birds because then Vito Santero took good care of the roof for no extra money and it kept the ladies off. The ladies didn't like birds.

On Sunday, Rosina Scarpacci came home from church to find a pigeon sitting on the footboard of her mahogany double bed, the one she had brought with her from Naples, her mother's marriage bed, the bed Rosina Scarpacci had been born in.

This was the worst of omens for Rosina Scarpacci, who believed in omens. She made her living conjuring spells. Rosina Scarpacci was not Donna Vecchio, but she was still a woman of power.

When she saw the bird in her bedroom that Sunday morning, Rosina Scarpacci screamed through the hallways. She screamed that her end was near, the angel of death perched on the footboard of her bed. She collapsed on the second-floor landing.

The building emptied out. Joey Dee's father was home, since it was Sunday, and Rosina Scarpacci woke him up with her screams outside his door. He came out into the hallway. Aunt Julia came out from her door across the landing and the two of them stood over Rosina Scarpacci, whose screams were fading into whimpers.

Aunt Julia waved a hand in the air and clicked her tongue

against the roof of her mouth when she saw who it was. Aunt Julia was not a believer. "I thought something important was happening." she said, and went back inside.

"*Puttana!*" Rosina Scarpacci called after her. "Why aren't you in church?" she said, and swooned again. Aunt Julia slammed her door.

Joey Dee's father reached down to help Rosina Scarpacci. "Forgive me, I know . . . your sister," she said, clutching at his arm. "The bird . . . on my bed." The wide brim of her hat was bent. She held herself against Joey Dee's father and tried to get up. He had no shirt on. Rosina Scarpacci fell back when she touched his bare skin. She sat down on the floor, put her head in her hands, and moaned.

"Stay here, Donna Rosina," Joey Dee's father said. "I'll go up and see."

Joey Dee came home from church and Rosina Scarpacci looked up at him. "It's your bird on my bed," she said, "yours . . ."

"We'll get the bird, Donna Rosina. You just relax," Joey Dee's father said. He took Joey Dee by the back of the neck and they went up the stairs together to Rosina Scarpacci's apartment. The bird had moved to the headboard and it tilted its head when it saw Joey Dee.

It was a silver baldy. Joey Dee knew his birds. He knew by the size of the crest on its beak that it was an old one. He had had it a long time. "It's not mine," he told his father. "I keep mine on Sammy One-eye's roof. Why would one of my birds come all the way down to Spring Street? It must be one of Willie's. He's got birds next door. The old witch is just trying to get me in trouble."

Joey Dee's father put his hand on his son's shoulder and spoke into his ear. "It's got a yellow band on its leg. It's yours. Now get the bird and get it out of here before I wring its neck." Joey Dee caught the bird and held it against his chest. "You're always making trouble," his father said. "You almost gave Rosina a heart attack with this goddamn bird."

Joey Dee put the bird inside his jacket. "Since when you're

so worried about Rosina Scarpacci?" he said. "You're the one always calling her an old witch. She gets mad at me, all of a sudden she's 'Donna Rosina.' What's the big deal, the bird came in her bedroom? She left the window open."

"Get rid of the birds," his father said, "all of them, and get a job." Joey Dee followed his father downstairs. "A job," he kept saying. "Get a job."

Rosina Scarpacci was sitting in the kitchen, drinking coffee with Joey Dee's mother. Her hat was straight on her head, but the brim was bent forever. "She's fine now," Joey Dee's mother said, patting her arm.

"The birds are going, Donna Rosina," Joey Dee's father told her. "This won't happen again. Don't worry." Rosina looked at Joey Dee, her mouth small and tight.

Joey Dee left the house with the pigeon inside his jacket. His mother called after him but he wouldn't answer. He found Mikey Bats and Carmine on the corner of the church and told them about Rosina Scarpacci and asked if they would help him take away the birds. He asked Carmine to take him in his car.

Carmine said he would meet him downstairs in front of Sammy One-eye's building with the car. Joey Dee went up the roof and gathered the birds in boxes. He talked to them, he petted them. He was glad Vito Santero wasn't around to see what he was doing. Mikey Bats came up the roof to help him carry down the boxes.

"Where to?" Carmine said when they were all in the car.

"Out Long Island," Joey Dee told him. "I got a cousin near Patchogue. He'll keep them for me." Joey Dee felt bad about the birds but good to be sitting in a car with his friends on his way out of the city. He sat back and rolled down the window.

"She's a witch, that Rosina Scarpacci, ain't she?" Mikey Bats said. "All them ladies are witches, with their big hats and their big mouths."

"You forgot their big knees," Carmine said. "You think they get them big knees from sitting in the park all the time?"

"Nah," Mikey Bats said. "It's from the garters. Those garters they wear push everything up."

"Garters are sexy," Carmine said. "On the right girl, garters are something wonderful." When Carmine said this, Joey Dee thought of Josie Magro, Josie Magro with Carmine. Josie Magro wore garters with pink satin flowers near the edge of them. He remembered how when he put his hand up her leg, her skin felt as smooth as the satin. He pushed the thought out of his head and thought instead about his pigeons that he had to bring to Long Island because of Rosina Scarpacci. He wondered if women would always ruin his life.

It took hours to get to Patchogue. Pants pressers, Joey Dee thought, out for a Sunday drive with their families. He shifted in the backseat.

"I didn't know you were so crazy about those pigeons," Carmine said.

"Joey's had pigeons since he was a kid," Mikey Bats said.

"Some of the neighborhood guys keep them up the factory roofs on West Broadway," Carmine said. "Maybe you could put them up there."

"No," Joey Dee said. "I've got everything up Sammy One-eye's roof. When the old man cools down, I'll bring them back."

It was starting to get dark when they got back from Long Island and pulled up on Sullivan Street. Joey Dee got out of the car. He looked up at Sammy One-eye's building and saw his pigeons, all of them lined along the top of the building, waiting for him to come up and put them in their boxes so they could put their heads under their wings and shut out the world.

Joey Dee went in the building and up the stairs to the roof. Josie Magro was there, sitting against the parapet wall, the pigeons in a line above her head. She sat with her knees bent up and apart, her skirt high up on her legs. It was September but hot like August. She had soot on her face and under her nails.

"I've been waiting for you," she said. "What's going on with the birds?"

"Rosina Scarpacci," he said. "One went in her house, on her bed. I had to get rid of them. I took them out to Long Island."

"But they came back to you." she said. "When I got here the coop was empty, and then they all started coming from nowhere, lining up along the wall."

"I've got to put them away." He took off his suit jacket.

"Leave the birds out for a while. Come over here with me."

He looked at her. "What are you doing sitting on the roof?" he said. "I got a chair in here. Take the chair."

"I don't want the chair."

He shrugged. "You don't know what you want, Josie." He hung the jacket over the back of the chair he kept inside the pigeon coop. He straightened the shoulders and smoothed the lapels. "We've got to talk," he said.

"I don't want to talk. We never talk. We always fight. Come here," she said, "and don't ask me questions. You're always giving me the third degree. Just come down here. I'm so unhappy . . ."

They lay down together on the roof. Joey Dee kneeled over Josie Magro on the soft tar of the roof. The birds stayed on the parapet wall above them, the moonlight caught on their feathers.

After, he gave Josie Magro his white linen handkerchief to clean herself, but she said no, she didn't care, and he wondered how she couldn't. Joey Dee thought about his silk suit and the tar and soot on the roof, but he lay back as if he didn't care either. He looked up at the pigeons on the parapet wall.

"My mother told me a story about pigeons," she said. "What they would do with pigeons."

"Tell me."

"I can't. It's a secret."

"I keep secrets."

"It's a woman secret. I can't."

*   *   *

Carolina Magro had told Josie that women used the insides of a pigeon to trick a husband on the wedding night. Carolina Magro had laughed when she told her this. "The old ways," she had said, but she hadn't told Josie that she had learned this from Donna Vecchio.

Carolina Magro was Tommy California's girl when she said yes to Sonny Magro. Donna Vecchio knew this. She told Carolina that Sonny Magro would know on the wedding night. His mother would know the morning after. He would hold it against her her whole life, Donna Vecchio had said. The way was to take a pigeon . . . It was done all the time.

"No," Carolina had said. "This is America."

"Men are men," Donna Vecchio told her, but Carolina wouldn't listen.

Joey Dee reached across and touched Josie Magro. "Let's switch secrets," he said. "I'll go first."

"Go ahead."

"I'm crazy about you."

Josie Magro sat up. She put her arms around her knees.

"Tell me the woman secret," he said.

"There is none," Josie Magro said. "I was making it up."

TEN

Nicky Mole was drinking coffee at the table in the back of the cafe, behind the curtain. It was early in the morning and the cafe was empty except for Nicky Mole and the parrot, Santino, that Sammy One-eye had bought from a Genovese sailor in the Kiwi Bar on Houston Street. The parrot had a yellow-and-green head. "This bird's from darkest Africa," the sailor had told Sammy One-eye while he counted out the money.

When Sammy One-eye had walked past the cafe with the bird on his shoulder, Nicky Mole was standing outside. He watched Sammy One-eye until he had turned a corner and then he sent Benny Scar after him, to find him and buy his parrot. Benny Scar came back with the parrot in a cardboard box with openings punched along the sides like portholes. "A gift from Sammy One-eye," he told Nicky Mole.

Santino, Nicky Mole named the parrot, after a childhood friend who had died of typhus. It was hard to believe Nicky Mole had had a friend. It was hard to believe he had had a childhood. "Maybe a childhood," the ladies said, "but never a friend."

Nicky Mole had a gold chain made for Santino's leg. He would stroke Santino's head, and Santino would put his beak in Nicky Mole's hair. He would rub his head against Nicky Mole's ear and close his parrot eyes.

When Nicky Mole couldn't sleep, he would come to the cafe and sit at the table in the back behind the curtain. He would make himself coffee, and stroke Santino's head. He would talk to him like a lover, like a son. He would feed him fresh cherries that Fat Frankie brought from the docks when a ship came in.

Nicky Mole had always wanted a parrot for his own. When he was young, in the *bassi*, a man would come with a parrot who would tell your fortune for a coin. The parrot would pick a card with your destiny written on it from a wooden box hanging from the man's neck. It was dark in the *bassi*; the women wore black. The parrot was bright green. Not even the sea was so green.

This morning was one of those mornings when Nicky Mole couldn't sleep. It was just turning light when he made himself coffee and sat down to stroke Santino. In the old country, he told the parrot, it was easier to be a man of honor. It was clearer how men should behave. He petted Santino's beak.

"A black calf, its legs cut off, anyone could understand that," he said. "Red and black, blood and mourning, things made sense. Here . . . it's different."

The parrot moved to Nicky Mole's shoulder and pushed its beak in his hair where it was starting to gray at the temples. The parrot closed its eyes and stayed very still. Nicky Mole liked how Santino could sit so still. Nicky Mole admired stability.

Jumbo came in to set up the coffee. He was smiling this morning because he was leaving. A job on the Brooklyn piers had opened up. Thank God, he had said to his wife only this morning. No disrespect to Benny, he had added, but the cafe was no place for him. He didn't want to worry her, he said, but he had been losing weight.

Benny Scar and Fat Frankie came in and Nicky Mole called them into the back behind the curtain. He told Jumbo to go sit outside in the sun.

"I got guys coming with the vig, Nicky. I gotta be outside. They come early, before work," Benny Scar said.

Nicky Mole banged on the table. His coffee cup went over. Santino flew up squawking and settled on Fat Frankie, who hated the parrot and the way its talons dug into his shoulder. He could feel them even through the pads in his jacket, which the tailor had told him would make him look taller and trimmer.

"You think I would keep you here for nothing? We gotta talk . . . now." He stared at them for a while to make sure they were paying attention. "The *stunade*," he said finally, when he was convinced they were listening. "What's he doing? What's going on with him?"

"I don't know, Nicky." Fat Frankie said. He could hear his stomach making hungry, nervous noises. "But he's acting strange."

Nicky Mole drew back his hand but stopped himself. "Of course he acts strange. He's a *stunade*, no?"

"But he ain't acting like he usually does."

"Talk," Nicky Mole said. He stood up and put both his hands on the table. "I'm listening."

Fat Frankie pushed his chair back and put his hand in his suit pocket. It was full of peanuts he had taken from Santino's dish, but there was no way he could get them into his mouth. Fat Frankie fingered the peanuts. He rolled them around in his palm. "He told the priest . . ."

"So what, everybody tells the priest. The priest ain't supposed to talk, that's why everybody tells the priest." Nicky Mole knew all about priests. "What else?" he said, sitting back down.

". . . and he told that kid, Joey Dee. He told him first, before the priest, and now he's telling . . ."

"Telling who, Frankie . . . Who?"

". . . the pigeons."

Nicky Mole came out of his seat. He curled his hands into fists. "The pigeons, Frankie? The *stunade* is telling the pigeons?"

Benny Scar stood up and put a hand on Fat Frankie's shoulder. Fat Frankie threw a handful of peanuts in his mouth and sighed with relief. He chewed them quietly and let Benny Scar take over. He let Benny Scar talk. "He goes up the roof, boss, Sammy One-eye's roof, where the kid keeps his pigeons. He cleans the cages, hangs out with the birds, that's how come he was up there that night we got . . ."

"I still don't understand nothing," Nicky Mole said.

"So now he goes up the roof and he yells all about Sonny Magro getting it on the roof, word for word what happened, boss, and he says it over and over, and then he goes down the church and sits in the confession box and tells Giannini, over and over. He's always in that box blabbing about Sonny Magro. He calls it 'the story.' 'This is the story,' he says."

"Son of a bitch," Nicky Mole said. "The *stunade* had to see. If he wasn't a *stunade*, he would know not to talk. No one in his right mind would talk, so what do we get? A *stunade* . . ."

Fat Frankie sat up straight. "We can take care of him easy, boss," he said. Fat Frankie made his hands into fists and snapped them apart.

"You're a *stunade*, too," Nicky Mole told Fat Frankie. "You just gonna break his neck and leave him in the street next to those goddamn ashcans he's always rolling around? You gonna sit him in that chair? Throw him off the roof like the other one? Did you ever have a new idea?" He smacked Fat Frankie on the side of the head and Santino flew up again and onto his perch near the widow. Fat Frankie was grateful.

Benny Scar put his hand under his chin to show he was thinking. Nicky Mole walked over to Santino. "Tell these stupids, Santino, tell them what to do with the *stunade* who talks too much."

Santino started to sing. He sang a vulgar song from the port city of Genova, where the sailor who owned him had come from. He sang it in Genovese. It sounded like French to Nicky Mole. It sounded like Chinese. It convinced him the parrot was intelligent.

Nicky Mole turned around to face Benny Scar and Fat

Frankie "The roof," he said. "Get him up the roof . . . but this time make sure there's nobody up there but pigeons."

Fat Frankie stuffed the last of the peanuts and pocket lint into his mouth. "And we'll make him disappear, quiet-like, right, boss?"

"No," Nicky Mole said. "Not that. I made a promise to the priest. I swore to God—no innocents. They ain't responsible."

Fat Frankie was confused. He fished around in his pocket, but the peanuts were finished. He thought about the cream-filled swans in Canapa's window and the *focaccia* he could dunk in his coffee.

Benny Scar knew that when Nicky Mole talked about God or his mother, there was nothing to say. Even the boss had bosses.

"But what do we do then?" Fat Frankie said.

"We just shut him up." Nicky Mole took Santino on his wrist. He petted his beak with his finger. "Now, what about this kid, this Joey Dee?"

"He's got a closed mouth, that kid," Benny Scar said. "He's laying low, but he ain't talking. I got that other kid, Carmine Menotti on him, but he ain't saying nothing. I even got Menotti taking out the daughter."

"What daughter? What are you talking about?"

Suddenly Benny Scar didn't want to say anything else. He didn't want to say the wrong thing. He looked around as if there were someone in the room who could get him off the hook. "Josie Magro . . ." he said. "Joey Dee takes her out, but he keeps it real quiet. I thought he might have told her something, so I got this kid Carmine after her to see what he can find out, but so far nothing. Like I told you. He's a close-mouthed kid. I was trying to cover the bases, Nicky."

"The kid goes out with Josie Magro. How come I don't know this?"

"I just now found out, boss. But this kid ain't the problem. It's the *stunade*. He don't know what he's doing."

"Yeah," Nicky Mole said. "His bad luck and ours he's going crazy in the head. He should have two blind eyes instead of one."

"That bad eye ain't blind, boss," Fat Frankie said. "It just moves around, like it's loose or something."

Nicky Mole put Santino back on his perch. He wiped his forehead with a big white linen handkerchief. "Get that kid in here," he said to Benny Scar, "and get this guy out." He waved a hand at Fat Frankie. "And leave me alone," he said. "I gotta think."

When Joey Dee walked up Sullivan Street, men were putting up the poles that would hold the garlands shaped like flowers and the strings of electric lights for the festival of Saint Anthony. The festival was late this year, a natural disaster having occurred in the Bay of Naples. With reverence for the victims of the disaster, the celebrations had been postponed.

"An omen," the ladies said of the disaster. "Ill, of course." They crossed themselves when they passed the church, and kissed their fingers up to God.

There had been great discussions about the festival and the disaster in Naples. The festival must go on as planned. They must please the saint; they must honor him. Besides, these voices said, the disaster was over there, and we are over here. It has nothing to do with us.

But there were others who said the festival should be canceled, forgotten until next year. That was the right thing to do. Saint Anthony didn't want a festival, dancing in the street when his people were suffering. There was no difference between here and over there. They were all his sons.

Nicky Mole took great interest in the discussions. Every rice ball, every clam, every piece of *torrone* sold at the festival put money in Nicky Mole's pocket. He was behind the society that collected money in the name of the saint.

He met with the citizens: the ones for having the festival and the ones against. The meeting was held in the cafe on Sullivan Street. Food was brought in from the San Remo Restaurant.

There would be a festival, Nicky Mole told the citizens, and there would be a penance. The feast would be postponed until the fall. This would satisfy the Saint. The bandstand would be built high above the sidewalk as usual and there would be dancing in the block between Prince Street and Spring.

The citizens left the cafe with full stomachs and hearts. The old men kissed Nicky Mole's hand, although he modestly told them it was unnecessary. They mumbled among themselves about his wisdom and generosity.

Nicky Mole watched the string of lights go up and remembered the *bassi*, where lights were strung from one balcony to the other, around the shrines to the Virgin carved in the walls, and in the mouths of calves' heads over the butcher's doorways. He watched the lights and thought of the dark, under his mother's bed, under the earth. Life was sweet in this new country. He touched his ring, the sapphire blue and milky. He had bought Carolina an identical stone and had it set in diamonds for her fourth finger. She would be his, in the right way, as soon as he could manage it. He had promised her that, from the first afternoon in his office. He would clean away the past, he told her. The neighborhood would forget everything that had come before. Even the ladies on the park bench would forget. Every woman would wish to be her. He would make them wish this.

Joey Dee saw Josie Magro coming out of the mozzarella store. She had packages in her arms. He went up alongside her and put his hand in the middle of her back in a kind of embrace. She turned, saw it was him, and said hello. He could have been anybody the way she said hello and walked away. The ladies were watching from the park bench. They sat and fanned themselves with their handkerchiefs, their stockings rolled beneath their knees. It was September but hot like August. "Another omen," the ladies said. "Ill, of course."

Joey Dee walked up Sullivan Street in the opposite direction from Josie Magro. His face showed nothing. He crossed Houston Street and kept going north, all the way up to Fourteenth Street, to Hanley's Bar and Grill. Charlie Fish from the neighborhood was the bartender at Hanley's for a while now, and he asked Joey Dee if he was looking for a job. They might be looking for somebody, Charlie Fish said.

Joey Dee said he would think about it and let him know, and he thought to himself that he might consider it. It was dark inside the bar, cool and neon. Joey Dee forgot it was daytime and hot until someone came in and the door swung open.

Joey Dee thought he might like tending bar. He'd ruin his shoes, though. He looked down at the ones he had just bought. Aunt Julia had staked him the money. "Young boys need nice things," Aunt Julia said. "New things. Your father don't know shit about what young boys need."

Joey Dee had put his arms around her and she had laughed. He had gone straight to Eighth Street, to Siegel Brothers. He had put his spectator shoes away. They were only for summer and it was September. His mother had gotten the tar out of the little holes. She had done it with toothpicks when his father was out.

On his way back downtown, Joey Dee saw Carmine's car parked on Sixth Avenue. Josie Magro was in the front seat. She had her arms folded across her chest. Joey Dee stood there and watched her for just a minute before he opened the car door and slid behind the wheel.

"What the . . ." she said. Then she saw who it was. "What are you doing up here?"

"I could ask you the same thing," he said. "Give me the keys."

"What keys? What are you, crazy?"

"The car keys, Josie. Give me the car keys. I know Carmine didn't leave you sitting here without giving you the car keys."

"I don't have them."

"You do."

Josie Magro had her right hand in the pocket of her skirt. Joey Dee reached into her pocket. The keys were clenched in her fist and he opened her fingers and took them. He started the car. She pulled at his arm. She scratched at his face with her nails.

Joey Dee pushed her away and pulled the car out into the street. She sat against the door of the car and called him crazy. He wanted to tell her that she was the crazy one, everyone knew that, but instead he drove up Park Avenue and onto the East River Drive. He drove along the river. They didn't speak, even when he pulled off and parked by the side of the highway, in a place looking out over the water.

She moved next to him then. She put her arms around him and her tongue in his ear. "It's broad daylight," he said, but she didn't listen.

"Why don't you leave it alone?" she said to him on the way back.

"I don't believe you," he said. "We're fantastic. I'm crazy about you. I told you that."

"I like things the way they are," Josie Magro said.

"You're a real *puttana*, Josie. You know that?"

"So you keep saying. What are you going to tell Carmine about taking off in his car?"

"That's hot shit. What am I going to tell Carmine? You're my girl, Josie. Carmine should be worrying what he's going to tell me, like what you were doing sitting in his car on Fourteenth Street."

"Carmine don't know I'm your girl. Nobody does, remember? It's a big secret. It's such a big secret, it ain't even true."

"What do you want me to do? Pimp for Benny Scar like Carmine does?"

"I want you to leave me alone."

"You're full of shit," Joey Dee said. "You don't mean that." He put his hand up under her skirt. Josie Magro sat there as though his hand weren't on the inside of her leg. She looked out the side window of the car. Josie Magro had nothing on under her skirt.

"You're the one's full of shit," she said finally.

"Josie, you know how I feel about you. Don't play like some martyr."

"Let me out here," she said. "It's your problem what to do about the car. Carmine's probably telling Benny Scar about it right now."

They were stopped for a light somewhere in midtown. Joey Dee put his hand on the car door to keep her from getting out. "When will I see you again? For sure? I'm tired of taking my chances."

He got her to make a date, set a time and a place. He made promises. He said he would pick her up. He would take her to where Charlie Fish worked, where he was going to work. She would believe him. He would take her to the feast every night and they would slow dance together on Sullivan Street in front of the bandstand. He would dance only with her.

Joey Dee was still not convinced the neighborhood should know about him and Josie Magro, but his promises were real. It was his promises that made her agree. They were important. Joey Dee was not a guy who said things just like that.

He thought about tending bar at Hanley's, and having Josie Magro meet him there on Fourteenth Street on Saturday nights, waiting for him to get off. They wouldn't have to stay here, he thought. Josie Magro didn't need her mother, like the neighborhood girls did. She would go anywhere with him. Joey Dee thought all this after he let Josie Magro out of the car. He thought about the desert, the sun on his face. He left the car where Carmine would find it and walked home. He saw Vito Santero in front of Sammy One-eye's building and remembered that nothing would ever again be the way it was.

ELEVEN

On the sidewalk in front of Sammy One-eye's building, Vito Santero was sitting in his chair mumbling.

"What?" Joey Dee said. "Vito, what are you saying?"

"Up the roof, Joey, remember what I told you?"

Joey Dee looked around. The street was empty. It was early evening; the ladies were up the house. Next door, Vinny Canapa was turning up the awning over his bakery. "Vito, I keep telling you to forget about that. Maybe you should stay off the roof for a while. I'll get Carmine's brother to clean out the cages."

"You know what happened up there, right, Joey? I told you, didn't I? I told you and I told Father Giannini." Vito Santero shook his head. "What they did . . ." Vito's eye started to move crazy in his head. He tore at his hand with his fingernails. He twisted the edges of his coat in his fist.

"It's hot, Vito. Go upstairs and take off that coat, for Chrissakes."

Vito Santero reached out and grabbed Joey Dee's shirt in his hand. He pulled him down close to him and whispered in his ear. "I can't, Joey. I can't go upstairs. I ain't supposed to say nothing, but sometimes, up the house, I forget. I start talking and my mother says, 'What? What you saying Vito?' and I get scared 'cause I ain't supposed to say nothing. You told me that, Joey. Father Giannini told me that. First, he told me I didn't see nothing, but I kept telling him and telling him and then he said like you did, Joey. He said, don't tell, don't tell, don't tell."

"But you're not listening, are you, Vito?"

"I am. I am, Joey." Vito let go of Joey Dee and rocked back and forth in his chair.

Joey Dee stood up and smoothed his pants. He shook the crease straight. He put a hand on the back of Vito Santero's head for a moment, and then he walked away, down Sullivan Street toward home. The feast of St. Anthony was in full swing. The stands were open, the lights strung above Sullivan Street flickered on, and there were crowds of people everywhere.

Joey Dee turned the corner onto Spring Street and saw his father at the other end of the block coming home from work. He backtracked up Sullivan, past Nicky Mole's cafe, across Prince Street, past Vito Santero, who was rocking in his chair. Joey Dee went into Sammy One-eye's building and up the stairs to the roof. He opened the door to the pigeon coop and sat inside on the chair he had put there for Vito. Some of the birds flew to him. All of them made small, soft pigeon sounds. Joey Dee could hear the music from the feast down below in the street. He could make out people's voices, but only barely. He closed his eyes.

The crowds were gone by the time Joey Dee came down from the roof. Women with big arms were sweeping the street in front of the food stalls. The church was outlined in lights, the steps littered with losing raffle tickets. The band had packed up and gone home, but the gambling tent in the vacant lot was filled with people.

Somebody called Joey Dee by name. When he turned, he saw Benny Scar and Fat Frankie sitting at a table on the sidewalk near one of the fish stands. Fat Frankie was eating oysters. The empty shells were piled around the legs of his chair. Benny Scar called Joey Dee over with a wave of his hand. "Tomorrow night," he said when Joey Dee stood in front of him. "The car'll be on Varick Street. Where you been anyway? The boss has been asking. You got to be available, you want to do the right thing . . ."

"I can't tomorrow night, Benny. I can't, really. I got an appointment."

"Break it," Benny Scar said.

"Listen, Benny. I been meaning to talk to Nicky. I can't do this anymore . . ."

Benny Scar put hot sauce on a raw oyster. "The car's on Varick Street, kid. You got a problem, tell me some other time. Tonight I'm not listening."

Joey Dee thought about smacking Benny Scar off the chair, hitting him from behind. He saw himself kicking Fat Frankie in the groin when he came to Benny Scar's rescue. Then he would leave the neighborhood. He would take Josie Magro. They would go to Vegas and they would start out new.

"What time?" Joey Dee said.

"When are you going to get a job?" Joey Dee's father said when he got home.

"For God's sake," Joey Dee's mother said. "Shut up or change the subject. Give the kid a break. Talk about something else."

"There ain't nothing else," Joey Dee's father said. "He's a bum, and he's going to stay a bum until he gets a job or gets the hell out of here."

"I got a job," Joey Dee said.

"See," his mother said. "He's got a job. Now you can shut up."

"Where?" Joey Dee's father said. "Doing what?"

"Not pushing frozen chickens around," Joey Dee said.

"So what's the job, wise guy?"

"I'm the bartender at Hanley's, on Fourteenth Street. Charlie Fish got me the job, Angelina Lombardi's son-in-law."

"Another bum," Joey Dee's father said. "And Hanley's is Irish. What are you, nuts? Working in a donkey bar? Somebody's always getting hit on the head with a bottle."

"But you're never satisfied. It's a job, ain't it?" Joey Dee's mother said.

"Yeah," Joey Dee said, "better than pushing frozen chickens."

"That was a good job."

"Why don't you leave him alone?" Joey Dee's mother said. "You wanted him to get a job, he got a job. Now, what do you want?"

"I want to know where he gets his money, he don't work."

"I'm not gonna stay at Hanley's," Joey Dee said. He wanted to get off the subject of money. His mother's household dollars found their way into his pocket. Aunt Julia was always handing him twenty-dollar bills. Her men friends were generous, she said, and a young boy needed nice things. His father didn't need to know any of this, Joey Dee thought. It was none of his business. "I'm not staying in this neighborhood my whole life," Joey Dee said, getting up from the kitchen table, where the three of them were sitting. He stood behind his mother's chair and lit a cigarette.

"What's wrong with this neighborhood?" Joey Dee's father said. "Not good enough for you?"

"I asked you to leave him alone," Joey Dee's mother said. "How many times do I have to ask you?"

"When do you start?" his father said.

"Next Friday, but I might be filling in before. Charlie's gonna let me know."

Joey Dee's father shrugged. His mother took the ironing board and a Pepsi bottle with a sprinkler top out of a closet. She put the radio on, filled the bottle with water, and started dampening the pile of shirts that lay on the drainboard. She leaned over and kissed her son. "I'm proud of you," she said. "Don't mind him."

Joey Dee went down to stand on the stoop. Carmine drove by with Mikey Bats in the car. He waved and pulled over to the curb. "Hey, Joey!" Mikey Bats yelled out the window. "Come for a ride."

"Yeah," Carmine said, "you drive." He moved over to the middle, next to Mikey Bats.

Joey Dee got in and started the car. "What have you been doing?" he said to them, pulling the car out into Spring Street.

"We should be asking you that," Carmine said. "You're always just around the corner, out of sight."

Joey Dee didn't answer. Mikey Bats wanted to go to Third Street to hear some jazz, see some girls. Joey Dee liked the idea. In the Louisiana Club there was a girl called Beatrice who he hadn't seen in a long time. She was the color of coffee and wore feathers the color of parrots. Carmine said he wasn't in the mood.

"You worried about Josie Magro?" Mikey Bats said to Carmine.

Carmine made a face and waved his hand in the air. "What are you talking about?" he said, not looking for an answer.

"You believe this guy?" Mikey Bats said to Joey Dee. "Taking out Josie Magro?" He pushed his elbow into Carmine's side. "Is she really like they say, Carmine? Is she?"

"But you got no respect, Mikey," Carmine said. "She's a nice girl."

"Yeah," Joey Dee said. "A real nice girl. You seeing her, huh, Carmine? That's really something."

"She is *pazza*, though," Mikey Bats said. "Tell Joey what happened when you left her in the car on Fourteenth Street, Carmine, tell him."

"What?" Joey Dee said. "What happened?"

"You got a big mouth, Mikey, you know that. You're a little bit stupid, like Vito Santero. You're just like him."

"Hey, what's with that guy lately?" Mikey Bats said. "He's really going off, yelling up the roof all the time, mumbling in the street. My mother says he keeps it up, they're gonna have to put him away."

"Vito Santero can't hurt nobody," Joey Dee said. "He's a little slow, that's all. I swear, Mikey, pretty soon you're gonna be on that park bench full-time."

"Not me," Mikey Bats said. "You mean Carmine. He's gonna be sitting in the park with Josie Magro, holding hands."

"Forget Josie Magro," Joey Dee said. He smirked. "What about her mother?"

"You're telling me," Mikey Bats said. "But the word is she's with the Mole. Nicky Mole's got her."

"You belong on that park bench already," Carmine said. "Where the hell did you hear that? Your mother told you?"

"Don't give me that bullshit," Mikey Bats said. "You got ears. You didn't hear nothing? Maybe it's because your head's so far up Nicky Mole's ass—"

"Why don't you fuck off?" Carmine said.

"Why don't you tell me what Josie Magro did when you left her in the car on Fourteenth Street?" Joey Dee said.

"She's *pazza*, that girl," Mikey Bats said. "Tell him, Carmine."

"You want him to know so bad, why don't you tell him?" Carmine said. The three of them sat in the front seat of Carmine's green Chrysler, the three of them so close in the front seat that Joey Dee hardly had room to turn the wheel. They pushed against each other with every word, every gesture.

"He left her in the car with the keys, Joey. He comes back and she's gone. The car turns up on Sullivan Street two hours later with the keys in the ignition, and when he finds her, she won't say nothing. Tells him she don't know nothing and he should drop dead and stop bothering her."

"Pull over," Carmine said, "There's a spot."

"I thought you didn't want to go," Mikey Bats said.

"So now I do, so what?"

"Shut up," Joey Dee said. He backed the car in.

"Which joint are we going to, Joey?" Mikey Bats asked.

"The Louisiana Club."

"Why that one?"

"Why not?"

"You like dark meat?"

"You got a problem?" Joey Dee said.

"No, I'm just asking."

"We'll go out after the show. I know a girl in here, Beatrice. I'll get her to bring some friends and we can go up to Harlem to one of the clubs, unless . . ."

"Count me in," Mikey Bats said. "You in, Carmine?"

"I ain't going with no Zulu."

"Since when are you so particular who you go with?"

"What's that supposed to mean?"

"You're the one complaining about Zulus."

"I don't mean nothing. You wanna go, I'm in."

"Great," Mikey Bats said. "I'm sick to death of the girls in the neighborhood anyway."

"What are you talking about?" Carmine said. "You never had a neighborhood girl. You never had no girl."

"What do you know what I had?" Mikey Bats said. "What the hell do you know?"

"We gonna sit here all day or we gonna have a good time?" Joey Dee said.

"C'mon, let's go," Carmine said. He opened the car door and the three of them got out.

Inside, Joey Dee sent a note to Beatrice, who said she'd be outside the club after the show with Hortense and Louise and they could all go uptown.

*   *   *

When Joey Dee got home that morning he told his mother he had started his job. "How was it, Baby?" Joey Dee's mother said.

"Rough," Joey Dee said.

She kissed him and held his head in her hands. She put him in her bed so he could sleep, and when her neighbor knocked, she wouldn't let her in. "My son," she told Josefina Di Nardo, "works nights."

Joey Dee woke up late in the afternoon and remembered that tonight he had to pick up Carolina Magro. He had to meet Josie Magro tonight. His mother brought him coffee in bed and sat down next to him. She put extra pillows behind his back. "How you gonna do this every night?" she asked him.

"I just gotta get used to it," he told her. "Lotsa guys work nights."

Joey Dee's mother touched his face. She wiped the corners of his mouth with the edge of the handkerchief she took from under her sleeve, high on her arm.

Joey Dee thought about Carolina Magro and Josie Magro and sat back in bed and stared. His mother smoothed his hair behind his ears with her fingers.

Vito Santero's chair was empty when Joey Dee walked up Sullivan Street. Angelina Lombardi called from the window that Vito was up the roof. The pigeons were out, she said. She could see them circling in the sky and she could hear Vito Santero. He was walking back and forth on her head.

Nicky Mole was in the back of the cafe talking to Santino. He stood with the parrot on his forearm looking out through the barred window at the backyard of the cafe. He thought he should make it green out this window. He should bring in dirt and grow tomatoes and basil and figs. In the *bassi*, he had imagined a country estate. He would have flown falcons. His life would have been different. Who could account for fate? Nicky Mole touched the sapphire ring. He thought of Carolina and how he saw her only in darkness.

The car was on Varick Street the way Benny Scar had said. The keys were under the floor mat, and when Joey Dee unlocked the glove compartment, he found the directions to a place on Long Island. Joey Dee drove the car around to Sullivan Street and parked outside the church across from Sammy One-eye's building. Carolina Magro, he thought, was upstairs getting ready to meet him.

Carolina Magro came out of the building, her arms crossed in front of her as though she were holding the pieces of herself together. Joey Dee was never prepared for the sight of her, for the red of her mouth, the gold bracelet circling her ankle. They didn't talk. When she would catch his eye in the mirror, he would look away.

He drove her out to Long Island and waited for her outside like he always did, waited for her with his eyes closed, making up pictures of himself in the desert.

It was almost dawn when he came home. His mother called out to him when he opened the door to make sure it was him, to know that she could finally close her eyes now that he was home. His father snored. No one complained about the hour. He was working nights. The vice of his late hours had become a virtue. Joey Dee slipped under the sheets and wondered why he hadn't thought of a night job sooner.

With his father off his back and his mother content, Joey Dee pushed Josie Magro into the back of his mind. He knew she was angry. She would give him a hard time. He had broken their appointment. There was nothing he could say or do to change that. He couldn't explain anything.

He told himself it was better this way. He could make up with her after the feast. He told himself that her mother was a whore who went with wise guys. It's in the blood, his mother always said. Joey Dee half-believed it.

He went up the roof to fly the birds. Joey Dee sent them higher and higher. He made big circles in the air with the stick, and when they came down he counted them and put them in their boxes, two by two. But the roof was not the refuge it had been, the place where he could escape the life that was preordained for someone like him.

The serenity of the roof had been wiped away, like he had promised Josie Magro he would wipe away the past. Clean, away, he had told her, making an arc in the air with his hand.

When Joey Dee came down from the roof, he saw Fat Frankie and Vito Santero in the narrow strip of alley that led to the backyard of Sammy One-eye's building. Fat Frankie leaned over Vito. He hid him with the bulk of his body. Fat Frankie stood with his feet apart, and in the space between Fat Frankie's legs Joey Dee could see Vito Santero's broken shoes.

Joey Dee crossed the street and walked into Benny Scar, who stood near the steps of the church. He was waiting for Fat Frankie, Joey Dee knew. Benny Scar held his arm out to keep Joey Dee from passing. "Nicky wants to see you," he said.

Joey Dee stopped and turned to face Benny Scar. "Forget what I said about the driving, Benny. I don't mind. You can tell Nicky that."

"I didn't say anything about driving."

"So what does Nicky want?" The stupidity of the question stood in the air between them. Joey Dee knew better than to weaken his position like that . . . He should be holding up, keeping face.

"Nicky wants you to stop by," Benny Scar said. "That's all I know."

"What do you guys want with Vito?" Joey Dee said. He felt himself sinking in deeper.

Benny Scar shrugged and some of his scar disappeared into his shirt collar. Benny Scar did not have much of a neck. He walked a few steps away as if to tell Joey Dee that the conversation was over, but Joey Dee followed him and touched his arm. Joey Dee watched the scar change color.

"What's Vito Santero got to do with anything?" Joey Dee said.

"I don't know, kid. Why? You know something about Vito Santero? Something interesting about him?"

Joey Dee looked away, over at the ladies on the park bench. Their heads were together. They sat against each other, like his pigeons, making soft, low noises, their bodies touching.

He walked away from Benny Scar, feeling sick to his stomach. He crossed Houston Street and started uptown, ending up in Hanley's, where Charlie Fish said that if Joey Dee still wanted a job he could have his, because he was leaving. He was going to work in Nicky Mole's cafe. Joey Dee said he'd think about it and drank vodka with beer chasers until it wasn't daylight anymore.

He went to find Beatrice, who said he was too drunk, but she let him sleep it off in her dressing room until she finished work. Beatrice woke him up and said she'd drive him home, but Joey Dee was afraid someone would see. He was always afraid of this. In the neighborhood someone would always see, and that was the beginning of trouble.

His mother was buying the working-late-nights story, but he could hear his father through the wall.

"He's drunk," Joey Dee heard his father say. "The kid can't handle himself. He hasn't got the brains God gave him."

"Go to sleep," Joey Dee's mother said, and then it was quiet.

TWELVE

The next day Joey Dee felt sick, worse than when he saw the tear in Benny Scar's cheek change color. In the street, the hydrants were open, the garbage from the feast pushed into piles near the sewer drains. At the food stalls, rice balls sat in the sun. The cannoli cream curdled. It was October and shouldn't have been so hot, and Joey Dee shouldn't have been on his way to church at two in the afternoon.

Joey Dee wanted to light three candles, but because of the feast every candle in front of every saint was lit. He walked up both aisles and across the front of the main altar looking for candles to light, dollar candles, three together.

He found them finally in front of Saint Lucy. He had never paid much attention to Saint Lucy, a girls' saint, he thought, but he looked at her differently today, at the way she held the brown glass eyes out to him on a plate. Maybe she had saved these three candles for him to light, so he would notice her. Joey Dee lit the three candles and asked Saint Lucy to take care of things, to take care of Vito Santero. She should have a special feeling for Vito Santero, Joey Dee told Saint Lucy. She was the patron saint of eyes and Vito Santero had a messed-up eye. He told Saint Lucy about Vito Santero's eye in case she didn't know, and then he pushed three dollars into the tin box under the candle stand and looked around for Father Giannini's name over the confessional.

When Joey Dee found it, he had to wait. There were feet showing under the velvet curtain on both sides of the confessional. Father Giannini was in the center behind the lattice door. His nameplate was in the slot under the red light, lit to show he was inside, that sins were being forgiven. Father Giannini gave long penances. He asked questions about sex, long lists of questions. Young people avoided Father Giannini's confessional box if they could, but the ladies loved him. He never rushed. It took a long time to have your sins forgiven with Father Giannini.

Carmine had gone into the confessional box once, not behind the velvet curtains but in the center, where the priest sat. He had gone inside and turned on the red light and sat behind the grate and heard the sins of the women of the Saint Ann's Society who came to confession on Tuesday afternoons after their meeting. When Carmine came out of the confessional, he told Joey Dee that there were things going on behind closed doors that Joey Dee couldn't begin to imagine.

"Vito Santero's mother is humping Sammy One-eye," Carmine told Joey Dee. "'For the rent, Father.' Her exact words, I swear it," Carmine said. "And Genny Porcelli's daughter spent a weekend on West Twelfth Street with a girl who wears men's shoes."

Joey Dee wondered if his Aunt Julia was a member of the Saint Ann's Society. He told Carmine to stop, but Mikey Bats had wanted to hear more.

Joey Dee waited in the pew until both sides of Father Giannini's confessional were empty before he went in. He knelt on the velvet kneeler. Father Giannini slid back the door on his side of the grate. Joey Dee could see his outline, how he sat sideways with his hand covering his face, his fingers touching his forehead.

"Bless me, Father, for I have sinned . . ."

"Yes," Father Giannini said. "Go on."

"It's me, Father. Joey De Stefano."

"Your sins . . ." Father Giannini said.

"I have to talk to you, Father. You have to help me." Through the grate, Joey Dee could see Father Giannini turn and take his hand away from his face.

"What is it?" Father Giannini said. "What have you done?"

"It's not me, Father. It's Vito Santero. You know Vito, the dopey one who hangs outside Sammy One-eye's building."

"We are all God's creatures," Father Giannini said.

"He has to get out of the neighborhood, Father. You have to find a place for him to go."

"Why . . . ?"

"Something's going to happen. He saw something he wasn't supposed to see and he's talking about it and it's making some people nervous. You understand me, Father?"

"There's nothing to worry about," Father Giannini said.

"Listen, Father, Fat Frankie and Benny Scar had Vito Santero in the alley yesterday. What do you think they wanted with him?"

"I think you're exaggerating, getting overly excited about something that is really under control," Father Giannini said.

"They'll kill Vito."

"They will not kill him. That I can promise you."

"You've got to do something."

"What can I do?"

"Find a place for him upstate, one of the nun houses or a monastery. You can do that. Vito can work."

"The boy has a mother."

"His mother would be glad," Joey Dee said. "His mother would be real glad. I'll talk to her. Just set up a place for him to go and I'll get him there."

"I don't see how . . ."

Joey Dee put his two hands against the grate. He took a breath before he spoke. "Father, do you remember Sister Agnes? In the sacristy? Before the funeral Masses? Do you remember what she did in there?"

"I think that's enough."

"When, Father?"

"Come tomorrow," Father Giannini said.

"Thanks," Joey Dee said.

"What about your confession?"

"Tomorrow, Father. You got a crowd waiting out there."

The ladies were lined up outside along the church pews. They watched Joey Dee leave. "What a long time he took in there," they said to one another. "Wouldn't you just know?"

Joey Dee touched the plaster hem of Saint Lucy's robe on the way out and crossed himself.

Joey Dee avoided the block of Sullivan Street between Spring and Prince, where the cafe was. He didn't want to see Nicky Mole until he had straightened out with Father Giannini about Vito Santero. To get to Sammy One-eye's building, he cut through the alley on Thompson Street.

Vito Santero was up the roof cleaning out the pigeon coops. Some of the birds were out in the sun on the parapet wall. Joey Dee took out the chair he hid in the pigeon house and sat down.

"Sammy don't like nothing with legs on the roof, Joey," Vito Santero said, pointing to the chair Joey Dee was sitting on.

"I know, Vito. That's why I keep the chair in the pigeon house, where Sammy One-eye can't see it."

"But he can see the holes. He told me he can tell if somebody uses a chair on his roof."

"There's no holes. Don't worry."

"It's nice up here, ain't it, Joey. The birds is nice. You got so many now. You got a lot of new ones. You worried about losing them?"

"No," Joey Dee said. He leaned back in the chair, tilted it against the parapet wall. The back legs of the chair dug into the tar of Sammy One-eye's roof. "If you keep them inside for three weeks, they're yours. Birds are like girls, Vito. They forget fast. You know that, don't you?"

Vito Santero put his head down, embarrassed. Girls embarrassed him. They teased him and ran away when he came near them. "The only girl I like is that Josie," he told Joey Dee. "She's nice, I like her. Not her mother. I don't like her mother."

"What do you know, Vito? You don't know anything." Vito Santero's bad eye, the left one, moved slowly in his head, around and around. It made Joey Dee dizzy to look at it.

"You want the pigeons to sit on you, Vito?" Joey Dee said. Vito Santero nodded his head yes and sat down next to Joey Dee with his back against the parapet wall. He held his arms out straight.

Joey Dee went into the pigeon house and scooped up birdseed. He spread it along Vito Santero's arms and shoulders. He put birdseed on Vito Santero's head. He stepped back to admire him. "That looks good, Vito. We should take a picture."

"More, Joey. Put some on my legs."

The birds flew down and pecked at the seed Joey Dee had put on Vito Santero. The birds covered Vito's head and shoulders and arms and legs. "I look like a tree, Joey. A tree on a roof, a bird tree."

"You like trees and birds, don't you Vito?"

"Yeah, yeah, I do."

"What about living in the country, Vito? Would you like that? Being in the country with the trees and the birds? Wouldn't that be something?"

"Yeah, Joey. That'd be something."

"You want to do that?"

"How, Joey, how? Why you fooling me?"

"Maybe I can fix it, Vito. But you have to promise me you'll go."

Vito Santero moved and the birds scattered. He got to his knees. "Go where, Joey? With Sister Agnes?"

"Sure, why not? You'd like that, huh? Being with Sister Agnes?"

"Yeah, Joey." Vito Santero stood up. He smiled at Joey Dee, but then he screwed up his face, twisted it into a frown. He put his hand in his mouth. "My mother, Joey. What about my mother? Can my mother come?"

"She can visit, Vito." Vito Santero pulled up his shoulders when Joey Dee said this. The collar of his coat touched his ears. "Listen," Joey Dee said. "You can't stay with your mother forever. Nobody can. It's not healthy. You got to get out on your own." Joey Dee leaned over close to Vito. "What do you think?"

Vito Santero started to cry. His left eye moved crazy in his head. His nose ran and he wiped it all over his face with the sleeve of his overcoat.

Joey Dee sat back down in the chair and covered his face with his hands. "Saint Lucy," he said, "help me . . ."

"What?" Vito said. "What?"

"Nothing, Vito." Joey Dee sat up and ran his hands through his hair, smoothing it back close to his head. His hair shone black in the sun, coated in brilliantine, shiny like the feathers of a black bird.

"I can't leave my mother," Vito said. "And Sammy One-eye. Who's gonna take care of the garbage? What about my chair? Can I take my chair?"

"For Chrissakes, Vito. Stop fooling around. You can't stay here anymore."

"Why, Joey? I live here. My mother pays rent."

Joey Dee jumped up from the chair. He took hold of Vito's coat. The fabric tore in his hands. The birds scattered, this time high above them. "What did Fat Frankie want?" Joey Dee said. "He was talking to you. What did he say?"

"When, Joey? I don't remember. I told you I get mixed

up." Vito Santero sniffed up what he couldn't wipe on his sleeve.

Joey Dee let go of him. He reached into a pocket and gave him a handkerchief.

"Thanks, Joey."

"Don't put it away, Vito. Blow your nose with it. For Chrissakes, when are you going to learn to blow your nose?"

Vito Santero sniffed along his arm, then wiped the handkerchief over his face. He turned away and walked into the pigeon house. He went into a corner where Joey Dee couldn't see him.

Joey Dee put his face up to the screen and looked inside. "I'm sorry, Vito. I really am. I'm just looking out for you. We're friends, right? Isn't that what friends do, look out for each other?"

Vito Santero put his head out the door.

"So, if I set it up, you'll go with me?" Joey Dee said.

"Sister Agnes'll be there?"

"Yeah."

"And you'll come to see me?"

"Yeah."

"And my mother?"

"Yeah."

"And—"

"For Chrissakes, Vito, don't push your luck."

Josie Magro was sitting on the stoop when Joey Dee came down from the roof. Carmine was standing on the bottom step looking up at her. He saw Joey Dee before she did.

"Joey," he said. "What's happening?"

Joey Dee stopped on the step Josie Magro sat on, but he looked past her. "Nothing much," he said. "You?"

"I can't complain. Your mother told me you're a bartender someplace uptown."

"Yeah, I am," Joey Dee said.

"How is it?"

"Not bad. It pays the rent."

"Talking rent," Carmine said, "I'm getting my own place on Downing Street, some guy Benny knows. My old lady's been driving me crazy lately. Figured it's time to get out on my own. Maybe you'd like to come in with me. What do you say? We could have some good times . . . no one to answer to . . ."

"Sounds good, Carmine. I'll let you know."

Joey Dee walked down a few steps and sat next to Josie Magro. "So how are you?" he said.

She shrugged. The blouse she wore had no sleeves and Joey Dee could see inside it through the armhole. Josie Magro had nothing on underneath her blouse. The three of them were silent. They watched the people buying food from the stands in the feast and taking chances on toasters and stuffed dolls.

"The feast don't seem the same, having it in October," Carmine said.

"It doesn't feel like October." Josie Magro wiped a hand across her forehead. She pulled her shirt away from her body and shook it. "It's as hot as August," she said.

Fat Frankie came up the street. He had a half-eaten sausage sandwich in one hand. There was a fried pepper on his chin. He walked by the stoop and he touched the brim of his hat to Josie Magro. He told Carmine that Benny was waiting for him. Fat Frankie walked by the church and made the sign of the cross. He kissed his fingers up to heaven. Fat Frankie was a religious man.

Joey Dee knew Carmine would leave soon to meet Benny Scar in Nicky Mole's cafe. The ladies would go home from the park to have lunch and maybe a nap. They would not eat in the feast but only from their own kitchens. Joey Dee would wait them all out until it was just him and Josie Magro in the ttest part of the afternoon sitting on the stoop of Sammy -eye's building looking out into the street.

otta go," Carmine said. "You going up the house?" he

said to Josie Magro. She didn't answer but looked away. Carmine bent down and kissed her cheek before he left.

When Carmine had gone, Joey Dee moved closer to Josie Magro. He moved along the step until his leg was touching hers. "Josie, that night I was supposed to meet you . . ."

"Forget it," she said. "I told you before. We don't make any sense, me and you." Josie Magro stood up and brushed off the back of her skirt. She turned and walked into the building. Joey Dee heard the hallway door close. He didn't go after her. He could only think of one thing at a time, he decided. He had to get Vito Santero out of the neighborhood.

Joey Dee stayed up the house that night. He told his mother he was off work. He lay on the couch in the living room and listened to the music from the band that played on Sullivan Street. The lights from the feast made a haze in the night sky. He could see it through the window. If he stood in the window and leaned out, he would see the bandstand. He would see Josie Magro dancing with Carmine, and Mikey Bats drinking beer. He would see the ladies in the church booths selling plaster saints and hollow crucifixes with candles inside, which Father Giannini needed to send your soul to heaven when you died in your bed. Joey Dee's living room window looked out over Sullivan Street, the last block of the feast where the band was.

At midnight, the band played from one end of the feast to the other and the stands closed down. The gambling tent in the vacant lot stayed open until morning.

Joey Dee didn't sleep. Somewhere out West, he thought, he could be sleeping like a baby, or driving a Cadillac with the top down, breathing the desert air.

He went to church the next afternoon. The red light was on over Father Giannini's name in the confessional near Saint

Lucy. Joey Dee stuffed a twenty-dollar bill in the tin box underneath the candle stand and lit every available candle. Saint Lucy was his.

He waited in the pew until Father Giannini was alone, until the ladies had all gone, back to the church stand and the tables where they sold raffle tickets. He went under the red velvet curtain on the left side of the box. Father Giannini slid back the door covering the grate.

"It's Joey De Stefano, Father."

"I have a place for him," Father Giannini said. "It's near Elmira. The Mother Superior agreed. Room and board, possibly a small stipend if he works out."

"When can I take him up?"

"You're sure he can take care of himself? He doesn't have any . . . problems? A convent is a house full of women, you know."

"Vito's a little boy, Father," Joey Dee said.

"What about his mother? Did you speak to her?"

"I will," Joey Dee said, but he wouldn't. He wanted to get Vito Santero far away from Sullivan Street without telling anyone.

Father Giannini pushed a folded piece of paper through the grate. "Give this to Mother Sevina when you get there," he said.

"Thanks, Father."

"Your confession?"

Joey Dee made the sign of the cross and lied about his sins.

THIRTEEN

Joey Dee came out into the light of the afternoon. He bought two sausage-and-pepper sandwiches from Johnny Mopo's stand, and when he didn't see Vito Santero outside Sammy One-eye's building he went into the hallway and up the roof.

Vito Santero was pacing back and forth, telling the story of what happened to Sonny Magro. The birds were out of their coops, lined up, their heads to one side, close to one another, bodies touching. Vito Santero was up to the part where they took Sonny Magro's pants.

Joey Dee shouted Vito's name. Vito Santero turned, his bad eye rolled in his head. "Take a break, will you?" Joey Dee said. "I brought you a sandwich from Johnny Mopo's stand." Vito Santero narrowed his eyes and stared at Joey Dee. "It's me, Vito, Joey . . . C'mon, stop it. I brought you a sausage sandwich."

Vito Santero came very close. He put his face up to Joey Dee's. His bad eye slowed down. He opened his mouth and made a sound that could have been a laugh, but Joey Dee would not have bet money on it. "Get me the chair out of the pigeon coop and come over and sit down," Joey Dee said.

He waited until Vito was sitting against the parapet wall, half the sandwich in his mouth. "I'm taking you to the country Monday, Vito. It's all set."

"Where?" Vito Santero sprayed peppers and onions when he said this. His chin was coated with red grease.

"Remember we talked about it? The country, with the trees and the birds?"

"Sister Agnes?"

"Yeah," Joey Dee said. "She can't wait to see you."

"She said that? She told you that?"

Joey Dee nodded. "She can't wait."

Vito Santero got up. He dropped what was left of the sandwich on the front of his coat. "I gotta tell my mother—"

Joey Dee held Vito Santero's arm. "No, you can't, Vito. It's a secret, just like the other one about Sonny Magro." Joey Dee spoke into Vito's Santero's ear. "It's another secret you can't tell nobody," he whispered.

"But my mother—"

"You didn't tell her about Sonny Magro, did you?"

"No, no, I swear. I didn't. I didn't tell nobody, Joey."

"This is the same kind of secret."

"You're mixing me up," Vito Santero said. His eyes watered. The bad eye went around in its socket.

"Take it easy, Vito. Remember I told you we all have to grow up and leave our mothers? It's what happens."

"Yeah, but . . . maybe she don't want me to go."

Joey Dee walked over to the edge of the wall and looked down the six stories to the street full of people, to the noise of the feast and the lights that were on even in the afternoon because it was the weekend. The roof was another world, the mythical kingdom in fairy tales, up the beanstalk, over the sea.

"You have to trust me, Vito. You can tell your mother, but not now."

"Sister Agnes is there?"

"Waiting for you."

"When's Monday?"

"The day after Sunday. The day after the feast ends.

"But I can see the procession? And the fireworks?"

"Sure. The procession's on Sunday. We leave the next day. You be out front early. Don't say nothing to nobody, and I'll come by and pick you up in the car."

"Just you and me, Joey?"

"You and me, Vito."

Vito Santero picked a fried onion off his sleeve and put it in his mouth. "Johnny Mopo makes a good sandwich, Joey," he said.

Coming down from the roof, Joey Dee didn't know why he didn't feel better. This was it; it was over. Vito Santero would be safe, out of the neighborhood, off Sullivan Street. Joey Dee could think about himself, think about the rest of his life.

But he saw walls falling, waiting to bury him under rubble. He had dreams and premonitions. If he had told his mother, she would have lit candles and left shallow dishes of holy water and oil in the corners of all the rooms. She would have called Rosina Scarpacci.

He should be thinking of moving out, he knew this. His dreams were of the desert, driving in a car with the top down in the desert. The car was always a Cadillac. It was always blue . . . baby blue, sky blue, powder blue, blue blue. The desert was always in bloom, like in the picture Mikey Bats had shown him in Rocky's barbershop of the naked girl in boots and a cowboy hat. Mikey Bats had pointed to the girl, but Joey Dee had seen the desert and the flowers on the cactus, flowers as big as the breasts of the girl Mikey Bats pointed to.

On his way out of the building, Joey Dee passed Josie Magro in the hallway. She smiled at him as though nothing had come before and nothing would come after, as though time was always new for her, and not the series of hinged events it was for him.

"Don't expect me to feel what you feel," she would say.

"It's in the blood," his mother would say.

Joey Dee stopped to let Josie Magro pass. He flattened himself against the slot in the tile wall where the postman left the mail, but Josie Magro didn't walk by.

She stopped in front of him and pressed herself against him until she knew, but when he put his hands on her back and asked in her ear, she backed away. "Another time," she said.

He watched her walk down the stoop through the glass of the hallway door that Vito Santero washed on Saturdays with a basin of vinegar and water. Her skirt was too tight, the slit in the back too high. Joey Dee was beginning to understand why Nicky Mole was doing things he had never done before, why Sonny Magro had been killed on a Sunday. Maybe his mother was right.

It was Sunday and the last day of the feast. The neighborhood was out in the streets, the buildings empty. The church had been filled this morning, every seat taken. They had stood along the side aisles and filled the back. The ladies wore their big hats tilted to one side. The feast was a success, Father Giannini announced from the pulpit, not a day of rain. Saint Anthony was pleased.

"A good year ahead," the ladies said under their hats. The neighborhood thought about which combination of numbers they would play. They thought about numbers all during the Mass. They would watch carefully for numbers in their dreams. They would note the numbers of hospital rooms when they visited friends and family.

The procession started on time. Joey Dee stood on the stoop of Sammy One-eye's building next to Vito Santero to watch it. Angelina Lombardi leaned out the window. The ladies stood along the outside of the park gossiping, covering their mouths with gloved hands.

Josie Magro came down from upstairs and stood next to Joey Dee, and then Carolina Magro appeared, barely dressed, her hair loose. She stood behind Josie Magro and close enough to Joey Dee to change his breathing, to make him shift his feet and move as carefully as he could away from her and from Josie. He put an arm around Vito Santero, who looked up at him and spit on his cheek when he smiled.

The saint came through on the shoulders of the men of the Society of Saint Anthony. Fat Frankie was the second on the left. He wiped the sweat off his forehead with a large white handkerchief. Everything of Fat Frankie's was large, specially made, custom cut.

The ladies watched Fat Frankie wipe his forehead. Under their hats, they spoke from the sides of their mouths into their hands. "Sins," they said, "make the statue heavier, like the Baby Jesus Saint Christopher carried across the river. Only Fat Frankie is sweating," they said and shook their heads.

The statue passed, sheaves of money pinned along the cloth behind it and along its robe. Carolina Magro put her hands on Josie Magro's shoulders and spoke into her ear. She told her how when she was a little girl, Donna Vecchio would give her a one-hundred-dollar bill to pin on the saint. She told her how the procession would stop and they would turn the saint to her, and the band would play louder while she climbed the ladder to pin the hundred-dollar bill on Saint Anthony's robe.

Carolina Magro kissed the shell of Josie Magro's ear. "You'll do that," she said to her. "Next year, the procession will stop—not here, not at this building, somewhere better—and you'll come down and pin the money on Saint Anthony, more money than any of them can afford, and the band will play for you." Josie Magro turned her head and touched Carolina Magro's fingers with her lips. Joey Dee watched them. They were the dark world of women, lit only by the moon.

Josie Magro leaned back against her mother. Carolina Magro turned Josie Magro's hair in her hands. Before Carolina had come down, Josie Magro had leaned against Joey Dee and touched him with promises, small promises that made him forget everything else, but now she was with her mother and Joey Dee stood alone.

"*Stregas*," the ladies said, watching them. They saw everything. They saw Josie Magro not as a girl anymore but as a woman, and their sympathy for her was gone.

Joey Dee saw Carmine on the other side of the street, and when the saint had been carried up into the church and down the center aisle, the whole neighborhood following, the ladies in their big hats in the lead, and Father Giannini waving the golden ball on a chain that sent out clouds of incense that made young girls think about the convent, Joey Dee left the stoop of Sammy One-eye's building and crossed over to Carmine.

Joey Dee asked Carmine to lend him his car on Monday. Anytime, Carmine said. He didn't ask Joey Dee for what. They were buddies. Joey Dee thought about their being buddies and about Carmine with Josie Magro and what did a girl matter between men, between buddies?

He wondered how much Josie Magro mattered to Carmine, but he didn't wonder for long, because if he did, he would have to get mad, he would have to get stupid. Joey Dee left that thought where it was.

Carmine said he'd leave the car in front of Sam and Al's candy store on Spring Street. He asked Joey Dee if he had thought about the apartment and the good times they could have. What about working with him? Carmine said. Benny always asked.

It wasn't a bad deal, Carmine told Joey Dee. It had to beat

bartending in that donkey bar and when did he work at Hanley's anyway? Carmine had been in to see him a couple of times and nobody knew who he was.

Joey Dee said he wasn't sure and maybe, he'd think about it, and that was strange about Hanley's, but Carmine should know the Irish weren't too bright. He thanked Carmine for the car and crossed the street.

Joey Dee went up the steps of the church and stood in the back. The church was full of smoke and flowers. The smell of incense burnt his nose and throat. A magic show, Joey Dee thought, then checked himself. He didn't like to tempt fate with disrespect. He asked Saint Lucy to intercede for him. He was getting to like her. Chances were good, he thought, that she would come through for him. She was the patron saint of eyes and not much else, and he was giving her all his attention. Joey Dee was partial to the underdog.

Nicky Mole was outside his cafe. He had crossed himself three times when the statue passed. Saint Anthony was his saint. He had worn his medal when he was under the earth, listening to the shovels full of dirt falling on his coffin. Nicky Mole's affection lay not with the underdog but with the man of power, the one carried on the shoulders of other men.

There would be fireworks in honor of Saint Anthony donated by Nicky Mole. They used to be set off from Sullivan Street, but Nicky Mole had moved the event down two blocks to Broome. He had insisted and Father Giannini had said it was a wonderful idea.

Nicky Mole never said why. He was not a man who had to explain. Not even Benny Scar and Fat Frankie knew the fireworks were moved because of Santino. The parrot hated the noise and the flashes of light. The first year, when the fireworks in honor of Saint Anthony were set off, Santino had spit up clods of cherries. He had picked out his feathers until the bottom of his cage was littered with them and there were bald spots under his wings.

Nicky Mole had the fireworks moved after that, and so every year, on the last day of the Feast of Saint Anthony, Santino slept in the back of the cafe, behind a black curtain, his head under his wing. Nicky Mole always closed the windows and the doors, even though the fireworks were three blocks away.

Joey Dee went to find Vito Santero to watch the fireworks. The stoop of Sammy One-eye's building was empty. Vito Santero's chair had been moved into the side alley. Joey Dee was about to look up the roof when he saw Josie Magro at the end of Sullivan Street.

She called to him and waved and he waited for her in front of Sammy One-eye's building.

"I've been looking for you," Josie Magro told him. "I called in the hallway for you and your Aunt Julia yelled down."

"What she'd say?"

"She said if you were up her ass, your feet would be sticking out. A real lady, Aunt Julia."

"What's that supposed to mean?" Joey Dee said. "Your family's so classy?"

"Forget it," Josie said. "Don't even start. It's always the same shit with you."

She was right, and that made Joey Dee mad and sad and confused. He touched her arm. "So why'd you come looking for me?"

"To watch the fireworks."

"Josie," Joey Dee said. "I want to talk to you, for real. We've got to make some plans."

Josie Magro shrugged off his arm. "I got my own plans," she said.

He wanted to hit her when she said this, for the way she said it. "Yeah, like what?"

"Look," she said. "They're starting."

Broome Street was wide and the fireworks rose over the factory buildings and threw down showers of light. When

Joey Dee and Josie Magro got there, Sammy One-eye had just finished putting up the silhouette of a woman who crouched in the sky, and with the next set of fireworks that exploded, the stream of stars came from between her legs. She peed into the sky and the crowd laughed and the ladies shook their heads and lowered their eyes. To each other they said they would bring this up with Father Giannini next year. When they looked up again, they looked high into the sky, above the silhouette of the woman peeing, to see the great balls of red light that shot down colors and made them ooh and ah with pleasure.

Josie Magro laughed at the woman peeing stars and Joey Dee put his hand under Josie's blouse. He stood behind her the way her mother had stood behind her during the procession of Saint Anthony and he kissed the inside of her ear where her mother had kissed it.

They walked back in the dark with the rest of the neighborhood who lived above Broome Street, all of them touching shoulders, whispering, shouting, a tribe walking through their territory in the dark.

"Take me somewhere," Josie Magro said. Her eyes reminded him of Carolina Magro's, the way they looked in the rearview mirror when he drove her to meet Nicky Mole, and he looked away.

"Where?" he said.

"The roof. Like the other time. We'll open the pigeon coop. Let the birds out."

They walked up Sullivan Street, and when she stopped in front of Sammy One-eye's building, he pulled her past it and up to Houston Street. He led her around to Thompson and they went through the back alleys and up the fire escape to the roof. Joey Dee kissed the backs of her legs as she stood on the ladder above him. It was dark when they climbed over onto the roof, moonless.

The pigeons were out. A line of them sat on the top of the

pigeon house. The door to the coop had been broken off, splintered. The wire mesh windows were torn open.

Joey Dee saw the dead birds. He saw the white ones first, white against the black tar of the roof, and when his eyes adjusted to the dark, he saw the others. He saw the blood. It stuck his feet to the roof. The blood formed a pool where the roof sloped.

Josie Magro covered her mouth. "What the hell is going on?" she said through the cup of her hands.

He told her he didn't know.

Josie Magro crossed herself. "Who could do this?" she said. "Why?"

He didn't know, he told her. He didn't know who had killed the pigeons and broken the coops and why there was so much blood. Too much blood for pigeons, he said.

Joey Dee kneeled down in the blood on the roof and picked up one of the birds. It was a homer, a white one. The blood and feathers stuck to his fingers. Joey Dee made a sound low in his throat.

Josie Magro came over to him. "Go down, Josie," he told her. She crouched down close to him, but he put his hand around the soft part of her arm and held her away. "Leave me alone," he said. "I'll look for you later."

Joey Dee thought he would throw up on the roof, in the pool of blood where the roof sloped. Vito Santero's blood, he was sure. While he was thinking about screwing Josie Magro, they had killed Vito Santero.

The fireworks, the whole neighborhood on Broome Street watching the fireworks. Where was Vito? "Can I see the fireworks?" he had said. "Will I be here for the fireworks?" Joey Dee couldn't remember seeing Vito Santero on Broome Street. Joey Dee had met Josie Magro and he had forgotten about Vito. He had left him on his own.

Joey Dee came down from the roof to the third floor. He stood in front of Vito Santero's apartment. The door was open and Joey Dee pushed it and went inside. There was a long foyer that led into the kitchen.

Vito Santero was there in the kitchen. He lay on a cot against the wall. Joey Dee thanked Saint Lucy. He thought he would get Carmine's car and take Vito Santero out of there right then. He would put him in the car and drive him up-state to Elmira. They would stop for breakfast. He would buy him a suit in the first town so he would look nice for the nuns. There would be a nun in the convent in Elmira who he would think was Sister Agnes.

Vito Santero had his face to the wall. Joey Dee went over and touched his shoulder. Vito turned. His left eye was moving crazy in his head. He had a rag in his hand and he held it against his mouth. A handkerchief, Joey Dee thought, a red handkerchief. Joey Dee pulled away Vito's hand. Vito's mouth was dark like up the roof and full of blood.

"Vito, what happened?" Joey Dee said. He pulled at Vito's arm. "Tell me," he said. Vito Santero tried to tell him. He tried, but he couldn't because he couldn't talk. They had cut out his tongue.

Vito Santero's mother stood in the entrance of the kitchen. "Vito," she said. "Why's the door open? What are you doing?" She came in and saw Joey Dee. "You have a friend over?" she said, and put her sweater on the back of a chair. "I'm late," she told Joey Dee. "I don't usually leave him at night, but sometimes I gotta get out. I was . . ." She looked over at Vito. "What's the matter?" she said. "What's wrong with him?"

Vito Santero was crying with no sound coming out. His bad eye rolled in his head. She saw the rag and the blood. "What happened?" she said, louder.

"They cut out his tongue," Joey Dee said.

"His tongue?" Vito Santero's mother started to scream. She hit Joey Dee with her fists. "Why?" she said. "What could he say? He's a goddamn retard, for Chrissakes. What could he say?" Vito Santero's mother pulled at her clothes. She ripped out handfuls of her hair and tore the buttons off her dress. Joey Dee put his head on Vito's chest and made a low sound in his throat that only Vito Santero could hear.

Joey Dee went back up the roof. The sun was coming up and he could see more dead birds, their feathers stuck in the blood that was drying on the roof, Vito Santero's blood.

Joey Dee went into the pigeon house and opened all the little doors. He let out all the birds that were left. He took the stick with the handkerchief tied to the end and spun it around and around, flying the birds higher and higher until they were so far up, he couldn't tell one bird from the other. Joey Dee watched them spread out over the buildings. He broke the stick in half and threw it off the roof into the back alley.

Joey Dee came down from the roof. He walked past Carolina Magro's door and Vito Santero's door and out into Sullivan Street. He went up the church steps and sat through the six o'clock Mass and the seven o'clock Mass and the eight and the nine. He wouldn't look at Saint Lucy. He thought he would sit there until he was an old man.

FOURTEEN

Joey Dee took Vito Santero upstate anyway. He cleaned him up as best he could and took him in Carmine's Chrysler. Sammy One-eye had taken Vito to the hospital, but the bleeding had stopped and they had told Sammy One-eye there wasn't much they could do.

Vito Santero's mother had his things packed in a cardboard suitcase she'd bought from the Jew on Essex Street. She told him to leave the coat without the buttons, but he wouldn't. Vito Santero put on the coat over the clean shirt Joey Dee's mother had pressed for Joey that morning, the shirt she had hung on the doorknob of the kitchen door, where she hung a pressed shirt every morning.

Vito Santero buttoned the shirt all the way up. It was too small and he struggled with the top button. Joey Dee had brought Vito Santero half a dozen white linen handkerchiefs, and he put these in the cardboard suitcase. The handkerchiefs had JD embroidered in one corner.

"I'll send you more," Joey Dee told him. "I'll have them made up with your initials, VS, in the corner in red silk, I promise."

Vito Santero started to cry. "He cries all the time now," his mother said.

Vito Santero's mother cursed the neighborhood. She cursed the God who had brought Vito into the world like this. It wasn't God, Joey Dee wanted to say, but he didn't. He wondered how she could have forgotten.

She kissed Vito good-bye and he held on to her. She took his hands from around her neck and told him to be good. Vito Santero cried going down the stairs and all the way up to Elmira. His bad eye never stopped moving. He sat in the front seat and curled his body in until Joey Dee thought his shoulders would touch in front, that he would squeeze out his heart.

The nuns at the motherhouse didn't care that Vito couldn't talk. They asked if he would take off the coat without the buttons, but Joey Dee explained that he couldn't. The nuns nodded and smiled.

Mother Sevina invited him for lunch, and Joey Dee stayed because he had never been inside a convent before, except for the parlor of the convent on Sullivan Street where Sister Agnes would make him wait sometimes. He remembered the Infant of Prague on the mantel dressed up like a doll in satin and velvet embroidered with gold. Every season Sister Agnes would change the clothes.

Joey Dee sat at the table with the nuns. He watched them eat. He never thought of them eating or sleeping or getting undressed. He never imagined they had bodies under their robes or hair under their starched veils. Mother Sevina didn't ask about Vito Santero's missing tongue. They ate lunch in silence. They spent many hours in silence, she told Joey Dee. They almost never talked, she said, except to God.

Joey Dee put an arm around Vito Santero and said good-bye. He wished him luck. "His eye," Mother Sevina said. "Does it always move like that?"

"I don't know," Joey Dee said.

"We'll take care of him," Mother Sevina said. She put a hand on Vito Santero's arm and smiled, a benevolent nun's smile, the smile painted on the statues that stood with their hands outstretched, palms open, promising the world, like Saint Lucy.

"You don't have a Sister Agnes here, do you?" Joey Dee asked just before he left.

Mother Sevina shook her head. "No," she said. "Never."

Joey Dee took Vito Santero's hand and held it. "You'll be fine, Vito. I'm going to send you those handkerchiefs."

Vito Santero cried.

When Joey Dee got back to the city, he parked Carmine's car back on Spring Street and left the keys with Sam and Al in the candy store. He stopped off at church to see Father Giannini, but he wasn't there.

Joey Dee planned to go up the house and tell his mother he didn't want to see anybody. He knew she would protect him from his father and from the outside. She would chase Josie Magro and Mikey Bats and Carmine if they came to call for him in the hallway. She would tell Aunt Julia to stay away. She would keep him tight and close inside the house and say he was sick if anyone asked. She would wrap alcohol rags around his head in case he was sick and fight with his father, who would say he was just a lazy bum.

But nothing was like before. When he came out from the church, Carmine was at the bottom of the steps. He stood with his body turned, looking down Sullivan Street, and Joey Dee knew he was waiting for him. He went down the steps slowly and stopped when he got to the bottom.

"Hey, Carmine, how's it going?"

"Joey, I didn't see you. What are you doing, hanging out in church?"

"Thanks again for the car," Joey Dee said. "It's back on Spring Street. I left the keys."

"Don't worry about it." Carmine shifted his weight. He moved closer to Joey Dee. He was uncomfortable, as though his collar was too tight or his balls were caught. "I got to talk to you, Joey."

They walked up to Houston and turned into the park where the ladies sat. They stood near the swings and Carmine held on to one of the poles. "Benny wants to see you, soon, now. I don't like to tell you these things, but what can I do? Better me, no?"

Joey Dee put a hand on Carmine's shoulder. "I know, Carmine. You got no choice. They tell you to do something, you gotta do it."

"You're a piece of shit, Joey, you know that? I'm your friend. Why do you keep giving me a hard time? I'm with these guys, that's my business. I don't see you knocking nothing off. You bullshit about some half-assed job in a donkey bar where nobody even knows who you are."

"Is that all you got to tell me? Or maybe since you're my friend, you can tell me what Benny Scar wants that's so important."

"That I don't know, Joey."

"You know about Vito Santero, Carmine? You know what happened to Vito?"

"No, what happened?"

"Nothing, nothing happened. You ask your friend Benny and you tell him I'll stop by the cafe this afternoon."

"You gonna be there, Joey? Don't make me look bad."

"Just tell Benny three o'clock."

The door to Nicky Mole's cafe was open, but the sign said KEEP OUT in four languages. Joey Dee went in and Benny Scar got up from his chair and came over to him. "Right on time, kid. I like that." He shook Joey Dee's hand. "Bring us some coffee in the back," he said to Charlie Fish, who was standing behind the counter.

Fat Frankie was at the table in the back, behind the curtain. He was eating a sandwich. Joey Dee could smell the cheese.

"Where's Nicky?" Joey Dee said. "I thought he wanted to see me." Charlie Fish brought the coffee in on a tray. He served Joey Dee last. They didn't speak.

Benny Scar waited until Charlie Fish had gone back through the curtain. "Who mentioned Nicky?" he said. "Nicky's not taking care of this. It's just me and Frankie."

Joey Dee didn't answer. Carmine had not said anything about Nicky Mole. Joey Dee had assumed. He was mistaken. He didn't tell Benny Scar this. Benny Scar did not care what Joey Dee assumed or what he had expected.

"Sit down, kid." Benny Scar pulled out a chair for him. There were three chairs around the table. Joey Dee's chair was between Benny Scar's and Fat Frankie's. Fat Frankie had put down his sandwich and was looking at Joey Dee.

Benny Scar leaned across the table. "Let's not fool around," he said. "You're a good kid, but you shouldn't be here."

"Like Vito Santero?" Joey Dee said.

Benny Scar didn't move an eyelash. The scar down the side of his face was white and silvery. "That was a shame," he said. "When I heard what happened to that poor kid, I felt terrible. Father Giannini told us you took him upstate, in the country. See, that was nice of you. You got a good heart. Nicky likes to hear things like that."

Fat Frankie nodded in agreement. His eyes drifted down to his sandwich and stayed there.

"What are you telling me, Benny?" Joey Dee said.

"You should leave the neighborhood is what I'm telling you. Go away for a while. We ain't just pushing you out, though. We want to help you get started someplace. We was thinking of Vegas. Good-looking young kid like you would love it out there. Plenty of action, beautiful girls. You could make a whole new life for yourself. What do you have here, kid? You got nothing. Am I right?"

Joey Dee wanted to laugh. They were sending him to Vegas, where he always wanted to go.

But he didn't want to go. Now that it was sitting in his lap, now that Nicky Mole was throwing it at him, all of it, he didn't want to go.

Benny Scar watched his face and waited. Sure, Benny, Joey Dee could say. That sounds great. There's one thing, though, just one thing I always wanted. A Cadillac, a convertible, baby blue. You know the blue I mean? Like the sky? Just that and I'd be in heaven. I'd never forget. I'd never thank you guys enough.

Benny Scar leaned back in his chair. "What do you say?"

"Suppose I say no?"

The scar on Benny Scar's face started to fill up with blood. Joey Dee thought he could see it throb. "I don't really think you should say that, kid," he said.

"I need some time."

"Like what?"

"Two weeks?"

"Two days. You leave tomorrow."

"I got things to do."

"You got nothing to do. You got nothing going for you. You should be on your knees. If it was my game, you wouldn't get Vegas, believe me. But like I said, Nicky thinks you got a good heart. He liked the way you took care of that Santero kid."

"What do I do?" Joey Dee said.

"Come back here tomorrow. I'll have everything ready for you. Come around eight, nine, when it's dark. You can leave from here."

Benny Scar pushed back his chair. Fat Frankie put the last bite of his sandwich in his mouth. Joey Dee stood up. Benny Scar smiled. The scar down his face had whitened. He called through the curtain for Charlie Fish to let Joey Dee out.

*   *   *

Joey Dee came out of the club and turned up Sullivan Street. He crossed Prince and Houston and kept walking until he reached Fourth Street Park. He went into the park and sat down on one of the benches. A pigeon flew down next to him. He thought it was a street rat at first, but when he looked again, he knew it was one of his. The pigeon moved its head from side to side. The sun caught the iridescent feathers that circled its neck. It was one of the birds he had raised up Sammy One-eye's roof. There was a yellow band on its left leg.

"What happened to Vito Santero wasn't your fault," the pigeon said to Joey Dee. "You did what you could. The nuns love him. They love affliction. God's innocent, they call him. And you, all your dreams are coming true. You can go away and see the flowers that bloom on cactus. You can have that Cadillac, the blue one you always wanted. You'll drive it in the desert with the top down. Lucky boy," the pigeon said, closing its eyes. "What a lucky boy."

If the ladies could see the pigeon, if they could hear the pigeon, they would bend their heads together and say what kind of an omen this pigeon was. An ill omen, the ladies would say. Birds always are.

Carolina Magro hated birds. She had told Joey Dee that one night when he had driven her far out into Long Island. She had told him that when they arrived and she heard Santino squawking. He loves that filthy bird like family, Carolina had said. Birds are ill omens, Carolina had told Joey Dee before she got out of the car. Donna Vecchio had taught her that.

"You're so lucky," the pigeon said to Joey Dee. "So, so lucky . . . lucky, lucky boy . . . all your dreams are coming true."

"You don't understand," Joey Dee told the pigeon. He moved along the bench and tried to grab it, to catch it in his fist, but it flew off. Joey Dee tried to follow it with his eyes, to see where it would go, but he lost it. It had had its say and was gone.

FIFTEEN

Benny Scar was right. Joey Dee didn't have much to do before he left. There was his mother, and there was Josie Magro.

He went to find Josie Magro. Maybe his dreams were all coming true. Maybe he just didn't realize it. He needed Josie Magro to find out.

Vito Santero's mother was on the stoop with Sammy One-eye. His hand was low on her back, his fingers caught under the waistband of her skirt. Joey Dee told her Vito was fine, the nuns were taking care of him, but she looked at Joey Dee as though he should be telling this to someone else. She looked at Joey Dee as though she didn't understand. He left them there on the stoop and went up to the roof. Joey Dee broke up what was left of the pigeon house. He piled the wood in one corner and left the feed on the inside landing. He would tell Willie to come and take what he wanted.

Joey Dee took out the chair he kept in

the pigeon house and sat down. He leaned back against the parapet wall. He would take Josie Magro to Vegas with him. He would tell her about her father and Nicky Mole and Vito Santero, or he wouldn't. He would tell her he loved her and they were going to Vegas to ride in the baby-blue, sky-blue, powder-blue Cadillac convertible he was going to buy. They would ride in the desert with the top down.

Joey Dee left the roof and went down to wait for Josie Magro. He stood on the stoop of Sammy One-eye's building and he watched for her to come. The ladies sat on the park bench and whispered in each others' ears. When Joey Dee went home, he told himself he still had tomorrow.

His mother was up the house alone. "I'm leaving," he told her.

"Now what?" she said. "Now what are you doing?"

"I'm going away. I got offered a job."

"What job? Where?" She leaned against the drainboard that covered the bathtub. "Where are you going?" she said.

"Las Vegas," Joey Dee said. "I got a job."

"You got a job uptown. Now you got a job in Las Vegas? Just like that, you're leaving everything and going to Las Vegas?"

"What, Ma? What am I leaving? I got nothing here. This is a score for me. I'm lucky to get it."

"But . . . just like that you're leaving?"

"I gotta go right away. That's part of it. They need me right away." He opened his closet and took out the shirts she had pressed for him. He put them on the knob of the door.

"You mixed up in something, Joey. You owe money? Tell me. You wouldn't be the first. These things happen. Look at Moe's mother, Graziana. She's in that factory on Wooster Street. Why do you think she works? Stands all day . . ."

"Ma . . . Nothing's wrong, Ma. I'm fine. I got a shot to make it someplace else and I'm going. That's all."

"Make it doing what? You're in trouble. I know. Mothers know these things."

Joey Dee stopped taking his things from the medicine cabinet over the kitchen sink. "Look at me," he said. "Everything's fine. It's all OK. When I get settled, I'll call you."

"Where? Where you gonna call me? We got no phone."

"Sam and Al's. I'll call you in there."

"Sam and Al's? So the whole neighborhood knows my business? So everyone will know before me?"

"Then I won't call Sam and Al's. I'll write. No one reads your mail, do they?"

Joey Dee's mother put her arms around him and her mouth against his ear. "I only had you, Joey. I only had the one. They all said I was crazy, having just one. 'Never,' Donna Vecchio said. 'One will kill you.' But I didn't listen, and now look what you're doing to me, what you're putting me through."

Joey Dee turned his face and kissed his mother's hair. "Ma, I'm not doing anything. I'm just trying to make a life. Why are you giving me all this shit?"

Joey Dee's mother pulled away from him. "Does it have anything to do with that dopey kid, Santero? The one you went to school with?"

"Where'd you get that from?"

"They took his tongue out the last night of the feast. Everybody knows that. And you took him someplace afterwards. Everybody knows that, too. Why? Where'd you take him?"

"Father Giannini asked me to do him a favor. He got Vito a job upstate in a convent. I drove him up there, that's all."

"I bet." She folded her arms across her chest. Joey Dee saw the handkerchief pushed up under the sleeve of her housedress, the scalloped edge against her upper arm. "When are you leaving?" she asked.

"I'm leaving now."

"You're not mixed up with that friend of yours? Not the slow one, the other one . . . Carmine. You're not with him, are you? He's connected. He's gotta be. He's always in that cafe. He's for sure connected."

"Christ, Ma, but you know everything?"

"What about your father?"

"What about him?"

"You gonna tell him?"

"You tell him."

"Me? I'm supposed to tell him?"

"I'm going, Ma." He kissed her good-bye. She held on to him. There was lipstick on his face when he went out the door. At the bottom of the stairs, he stopped and turned and looked back up through the slats of the banister. He kicked one of the ashcans that were lined up under the stairs. He kicked it out the back door and into the alley. He listened to it roll down the cement steps that led into the yard and then he left.

He went up to the hotel on Thirty-third Street and rented the room he always took with Josie Magro. He left his things and went back downtown to Sammy One-eye's building to find Josie. He waited there until he caught her walking into the hallway when it was already dark and everyone else was home eating dinner. He grabbed both her arms and told her she had to come with him.

He took her to the hotel on Thirty-third Street near Macy's, which is where she thought he meant when he said she had to come with him. But when he told her later, after, when the traffic outside on Thirty-third Street had thinned out and he had pulled up the shades so they could see the lights across Herald Square, she said she didn't know. She sat up in bed. "I don't think so," she said.

Joey Dee was going to tell her about her mother and Nicky Mole. He was going to tell her about her father on the roof of Sammy One-eye's building and about Vito Santero, but all he said to her was, "Please."

Josie Magro put on the face that he couldn't see through, the face he couldn't read, her mother's face.

"Come with me," Joey Dee said.

"Why are you going?"

"What does it matter? Don't you want to get away from here?"

"What happened to Vito?"

"Vito's upstate with the nuns. Father Giannini got him a job in the country. What's the big thing about Vito all of a sudden? Nobody cared if he was dead or alive, now everybody wants to know about Vito."

"You see, Joey, how full of shit you are? You never tell me anything."

"I'm sorry, Josie. I'm sorry," he said. "Listen, I'm going to Las Vegas. I'm leaving tomorrow. I didn't even say good-bye to my father. I'm gonna start all over. Come with me. I'll tell you everything, I promise. Let's just get out of here."

Josie Magro moved the pillows behind her back. She lit a cigarette from the one she was smoking and the red tip dropped on the bed and burned a small round hole in the sheet. It was something that long ago would have made him angry.

He waited for her to say yes. He would not believe that she would not say yes. He didn't know what he would do.

He waited until she had finished her cigarette and had pushed the stub of it into the ashtray beside the bed, then he came over and sat down next to her. "I'll pick you up tomorrow after it's dark," he told her. "I'll park the car across the street, by the church. We'll drive all night."

Josie Magro got out of bed and took a long time to get dressed. "When are you gonna answer me, Josie?" he said. "Yes or no?"

She looked over at him. "Yes," she said.

"Stay tonight," he said.

"I can't."

"I'll take you down."

"No," she said.

He watched by the window until he saw her come out of the hotel lobby and get in a cab. Maybe that pigeon in Fourth Street Park had really talked to him, had seen his future. Maybe he was a lucky, lucky boy.

Josie Magro went out into the street. She knew Joey Dee was watching her from the window. She hailed a cab and got in, but before she pulled the door closed she looked up to see if she could see him. She couldn't. There was a wall of windows and she couldn't find him. There were too many windows too far away, no time to search each window for a face, no time to count the floors, but she knew he was watching and that he would watch until the cab was out of sight and maybe longer.

Carolina Magro was in bed when Josie got home. She was asleep in the matrimonial bed that had belonged to the mother. The bed had come from the other side, from the old country. It was carved mahogany. Cherubs carrying ribbons met at the center of the headboard. It stood high off the floor on legs carved with roses.

The mother had told Carolina the story of the bed, of how her brother had given it to her when she married, of how his wife had objected.

"It was our mother's bed," her brother told his wife. "It belongs to her now. What else will she have?" Her brother was sad when he said this.

Carolina told the story of the bed to Josie the way the mother had told it to her.

Carolina had slept in this bed with the mother her whole life until she married Sonny Magro. She and the mother would fall together into the center of the bed and the mother would fit her body into Carolina's, her knees in the crook of Carolina's knees, her breasts against Carolina's back. They would lie there in the dark, like silver spoons in a drawer lined in velvet, and the mother would whisper into Carolina's ear. She did this when Sonny Magro proposed. He had come to see the mother. He had asked the mother to give him Carolina.

"Marry Sonny Magro," the mother had said that night. "Say yes. I tell you, it's the thing to do." She had whispered this into Carolina's ear. She had buried her face in Carolina's black hair, and she had told her what to do to secure her life. "A steady man, a steady job . . . no vices," she had told Carolina, "crazy for you, you will have him here in your underpants. Marry him," the mother had whispered into the darkness in the matrimonial bed that had come from the other side.

Josie Magro could hear Carolina's breath. She moved around the bedroom, opening drawers, taking things out. From under the bed she pulled the suitcase Carolina had bought for her honeymoon trip with Sonny Magro.

In the kitchen, Josie Magro took her hairbrush from the mirrored cabinet above the kitchen sink. She sat down at the table and folded her clothes and put them into the suitcase. When she was done, she snapped down the gold-colored clasps and ran her hands along the surface of the suitcase. It was old but still new because it had never been used. It had never gone anywhere.

Josie Magro stood at the window that faced out onto the street. She looked across at the church and counted the steps the way she had wanted to count the floors of the hotel from the cab window. She crossed into the bedroom and got into the bed with her mother. They had slept together in this bed, Carolina and Josie, mother and daughter, since that Sunday when Sonny Magro was found dead in the street in front of the church.

She got into bed and lay near the edge. She faced the wall and curled her hand under the mattress so she would not fall into the center. She held herself near the edge and closed her eyes. Josie Magro felt Carolina's body shift. She felt Carolina reach out for her, pulling her close, pulling her into the center of the bed. She felt Carolina's knees in the crook of her knees. She felt Carolina's breasts against her back.

"Listen to me, Josie," Carolina whispered. "Do as I say."

"I'm going," Josie Magro told her mother. "I'm leaving to-morrow, after it's dark."

Carolina tightened her arm around Josie Magro's waist. She held her close to her and spoke into her ear. Her breath was warm. "Trust me, Josie. Follow me. I'll never lead you wrong." Josie Magro touched her mother's hand where it held her waist. Carolina entwined her arm around Josie's arm. She grasped her hand and threaded her fingers through Josie's fingers. She put her cheek against Josie's cheek. "No one understands the way I do. No one ever will."

"I don't know," Josie Magro said.

"Yes, yes, you do. Say it. Say you'll listen. Say yes."

Josie Magro turned toward her mother. Carolina opened her arms. She held Josie Magro in the curve of her body. She stroked Josie Magro's head and petted her hair. She caught it in her fingers. They lay like this until the sun came into the room.

"Yes," Josie Magro said. "Yes."

The next morning Joey Dee duked the day manager at the hotel so he could stay until it was time to meet Benny Scar. He didn't want to go downtown again so he stayed in the hotel, ordering room service and smoking cigarettes. At six-thirty he got his things together and left.

Benny Scar opened the door of the cafe for Joey Dee and took him into the back room behind the curtain. He took out a sealed envelope and handed it to Joey Dee. "To get you started," he said. "The Buick's outside. It's yours."

Joey Dee took the keys from Benny Scar for the last time. He thought about his blue Cadillac and how he would ask for it, but he had no trump card. He wasn't holding anything. He was being spared. He was blessed. A new life in Vegas and a car to get him there. Lucky, lucky boy, the pigeon had said.

"When you get there," Benny Scar was saying, "go see Fortunata at the Desert Mirage Hotel. Tell him who you are and he'll take care of you. It's all set up."

"Thanks," Joey Dee said.

Benny Scar walked over to where Santino sat on the window ledge. He took the bird on his arm and stroked its head. Santino closed his eyes. "Frankie don't like this bird," he said. "A lot of people don't like birds. Me, I like them."

Joey Dee put the keys and the envelope in his pocket. Benny Scar turned around. "One other thing, kid," he said. "Don't come back for no visits. No trips for Christmas or nothing, you hear? Nicky's been good to you. Vegas is a score. It could of been Chicago or New Orleans. They ain't bad, but they ain't Vegas. So you go out there and you stay there."

Joey Dee stood with the keys and the envelope in his pocket and felt affection for Benny Scar. He felt grateful. He thought he would tell Benny Scar about the pigeon that had spoken to him in the park. Benny Scar liked birds. He thought he would ask him who had cut his face. He would tell him he was going to marry Josie Magro in one of those chapels in Las Vegas and would send him a picture.

Joey Dee wanted Benny Scar to hold his head in his hands and stroke him the way he stroked Santino, to talk to him softly, inaudibly. He put his hand out to Benny Scar. "Thanks, Benny," he said. "Thanks for everything."

Outside, Joey Dee got into the Buick and drove out to Calvary to see Sonny Magro's grave. The headstone was pink marble with flowers carved on the top and along the sides. Sonny Magro's name was carved into the stone with the dates of his birth and death. It was carved into the middle of the stone. There should have been room for another name on the stone, like there was room under the ground, room for a wife, for Carolina Magro, but Sonny Magro's name was carved in the middle of the stone. Carolina Magro was not going into this grave, not ever.

*   *   *

When Joey Dee got back into the city, it was late. He went to Sullivan Street to pick up Josie Magro. They would drive all night. He parked the car in front of the church, across from Sammy One-eye's building, and he waited. Vito Santero's chair had been put out with the garbage. Angelina Lombardi was in the window, her elbows on a pillow. It was still warm. It was like summer.

Joey Dee shut off the car motor and pressed on the horn. There weren't any lights in Josie Magro's window. Joey Dee pressed on the horn again, for a long time, until someone from Canapa's building yelled for him to stop.

He got out of the car and went up the stoop of Sammy One-eye's building. Angelina Lombardi saw him go in the building from her window, and when she told the story later she said she was surprised that he had stayed there for such a long time.

Joey Dee went up the stairs to the fifth floor and knocked on Josie Magro's door. Carolina Magro opened it. Joey Dee had forgotten how her mouth was too red and her hair was too black. He heard a door open on the floor below them.

"Josie . . ." he said.

"She's not here."

"Where is she, then?"

"Why don't you come in?"

"Just tell me where she is."

Other doors opened. Carolina Magro told him again to come in. "It's late," she said. "You want to stand out in the hall and entertain the neighborhood? Don't you know anything?"

Joey Dee came inside. He closed the door behind him and stood against it. Carolina had moved to the other side of the room. She was wearing black. Her dress had sequins embroidered on one shoulder. Her stockings were black. She wore black pearls around her neck. She was in mourning. She would be for at least a year. She had lost her husband.

Carolina Magro looked beautiful in black. Her mouth was very red. She was on her way out, dressed like that, Joey Dee thought, or just coming back. He wondered which.

"What do you want with Josie?" she said.

"I'm going away. She's coming with me."

Carolina put her hands on the sink behind her and leaned back. "Why don't you leave her alone?" she said. "Josie doesn't need a disappointed tough guy. She's not what you know. Josie's different, like my mother, like me. We've always been different. Some people just don't get put where they belong."

"So what happens?"

"They try to put it right."

"Is that what you're doing?"

"Why don't you get out of here?" she said.

"I can take care of Josie."

"I don't think so."

"You think I got nothing."

"I didn't say that. I think you got nothing for Josie. That's not the same thing. You should learn to listen. Anyway, she's not here. If she was going with you, she'd be here, wouldn't she?" Carolina Magro touched the diamond in her ear. She ran her hand down along her cheek and across her breast. "You in a hurry?" she said. "I don't have to leave for another hour."

Joey Dee came around the table. There was nothing left for him, nothing left for him to lose. He was free.

Carolina Magro opened her arms. "Put the bolt on the door," she said.

EPILOGUE

Carolina Magro married Nicky Mole. She did not spend the year in mourning. She did not wait the proper amount of time. The ladies talk about this, but Carolina Magro is beyond their reach. She is Carolina Malevento now. Donna Carolina, they must call her. She has left Sammy One-eye's building and moved to lower Fifth Avenue, off the park. The man who does her hair lives in the apartment. He serves her tea and small sandwiches in the late afternoon.

The wedding was quiet and far away. Nicky Mole picked her up late and they drove all night. They stopped at the first chapel. Carolina was wearing a black dress with sequins embroidered on one shoulder. Nicky Mole had her picture taken and said he would send it to his mother in the *bassi*. It would hang in every shop window, and the people would string lights around the picture of Fernando Malevento's bride the way they do around the Madonna.

After the wedding Carolina had curved her hand around Nicky Mole's ear. She had put her mouth close. "Josie," she had whispered. "What about Josie?"

When they got back, Father Giannini was summoned to the apartment on lower Fifth Avenue. "Of course," he told Nicky Mole. There are many ways into heaven, he would remind anyone who asked.

Father Giannini baptized Josie Magro. He baptized her in the eyes of God as Fernando Malevento's daughter. All the neighborhood came and there was a procession at the end. Nicky Mole gave out small gold coins and there were buns and cakes from Canapa's. Fat Frankie poured champagne.

The ladies objected to Josie Magro becoming Josie Malevento, to her being baptized twice, but they closed their fists around the gold coins and dunked the buns and cakes into their glasses of champagne. They bowed graciously to Donna Carolina, who had left Sullivan Street and Sammy One-eye's building the week before.

Nicky Mole walked home with his new family to lower Fifth Avenue. They walked through Fourth Street Park. Benny Scar and Fat Frankie were not far behind. They threw pieces of cake to the pigeons.

Mikey Bats was standing at the taxi stand outside the Desert Mirage Hotel when Joey Dee pulled up in a red Cadillac.

"Mikey," he said. "Get in."

"Jesus Christ, Joey. What the hell are you doing here? Nobody knew where you went. I kept asking around. What happened?"

Joey Dee shrugged. He pulled the car away from the curb. "I needed a change. A job came up out here so I took it. I didn't have time to say nothing." Joey Dee turned and touched Mikey Bats's face. "It's good to see you, Mikey. What are you doing out here? Can I drop you someplace?"

"I gotta go over to the Wayside. I'm with Benny now. Carmine got me in. Some guy in New York dropped a bundle and they sent me out here to square it."

"So you're doing good. How's Carmine?"

"Carmine? He's in tighter than a clam's ass. He's marrying Nicky Mole's daughter. The wedding's next week. The whole neighborhood's invited."

"Nicky Mole's got a daughter?"

"Shit, Joey, don't you know nothing? You don't get no news from the neighborhood?"

"No, I don't hear nothing. What's the point? I'm out here now. So what's this about Nicky Mole having a daughter?"

"The Mole married Carolina Magro, and he adopted Josie, so now she's Josie Malevento, and next week she's Josie Menotti. Like I said, Carmine's in tighter than a clam's ass, wears his hat pulled low to one side like Nicky Mole, gets manicures in Rocky's, tips big. You can't blame him. This is a nice car," Mikey Bats said. He ran his hand along the dashboard. "You always wanted a Cadillac, no? I remember you saying it."

"Yeah, but I wanted a blue one."

"Why? What's better than red?"

"I don't know. I just always wanted a blue one."

"Well, you know what they say." Mikey Bats shook his head. Joey Dee pulled the car in front of the Wayside Hotel and Casino. "This is terrific, Joey. Thanks. I'm not leaving till tomorrow. You want to get together?"

"That'd be great, Mikey, but I'm working tonight."

"The next time I come in, then. I'll be here a lot. These New York guys are always getting caught short. I'll see you next time."

"Sure," Joey Dee said. "Give my best to Carmine and Josie, will you?"

The line of cars behind Joey Dee started to lean on their horns. Mikey Bats went into the Wayside Hotel and Casino. Joey Dee waited until he couldn't see him anymore and then he drove away. He drove far out into the desert. It was in bloom and the cactuses were covered with flowers.

*   *   *

Josie Magro Malevento's wedding is the social event of the
year. The ladies say it will be bigger than Tommy California's funeral, bigger than the festival of Saint Anthony.

Carolina has ordered the lace for the dress from France.
The shoes are covered with beads. The newlyweds will live
in the building on lower Fifth Avenue, in an apartment across
the hall from Carolina's.

Everyone is invited to the wedding. The roses are coming
from Florida. The strawberries will be the size of fists, covered in chocolate.

The neighborhood has filled the church. There are more
people outside, crowding the steps, standing behind the railing
to leave the center clear for the bride. The first black limousine
pulls up and Carolina steps out. She holds the hem of her
gown. Her mouth is very red and her hair is very black. There
is a circle of diamonds around her left ankle. You can see it
when she lifts the hem of her gown. Carolina walks up the
steps slowly, one at a time. Benny Scar holds her arm. He
walks her down the center aisle to her place in the first pew.

Josie arrives in a second limousine. Her face is hidden behind layers of organdy and tulle. Nicky Mole is waiting at the
top of the church steps to walk her down the aisle, to give her
away. She is his daughter. The people throw petals from the
roses brought up from Florida.

Father Giannini is waiting at the altar with Carmine Menotti. Mikey Bats is the best man. He holds the ring. Nicky
Mole pushes away the veil covering Josie's face before he
kisses her and steps into the pew beside Carolina.

After the Mass, outside the church, the people throw pennies
and handfuls of rice. The whole neighborhood is there. The
whole neighborhood is invited to the reception in the Fifth
Avenue Hotel. The ladies say the wedding will go on all night.